475583LV0

MW00944400

EXPR:BW
PERFECT

475:                                    2]

*   L V U U U U 8 B A *

BOOK
SMALLWHITE

REWORK

mgonzalez:

Department	Operator's Name (Please print)
Printing	_____
Binding	_____
Cutting	_____
Shipping	_____
	_____

B2T Exceptions: 0/2

Printed at: Fri Feb 19 08:20:28 2016 on device lvoce04-86

Batch 475583LV00008BA

475583LVX00037BA	9780806300368	Historical Southern Families. In 23 Volum
PERFECT	5.50X8.50	284 (1)
475583LVX00072BA	9780806680712	Cómo Se Formó la Biblia
PERFECT	6.00X9.00	192 (1)

ISBN 978-1-332-09876-7
PIBN 10284401

This book is a reproduction of an important historical work. Forgotten Books uses
state-of-the-art technology to digitally reconstruct the work, preserving the original format
whilst repairing imperfections present in the aged copy. In rare cases, an imperfection in
the original, such as a blemish or missing page, may be replicated in our edition. We do,
however, repair the vast majority of imperfections successfully; any imperfections that
remain are intentionally left to preserve the state of such historical works.

1 MONTH OF
FREE
READING

at

www.ForgottenBooks.com

By purchasing this book you are eligible for one month membership to ForgottenBooks.com, giving you unlimited access to our entire collection of over 700,000 titles via our web site and mobile apps.

To claim your free month visit:

www.forgottenbooks.com/free284401

Similar Books Are Available from
www.forgottenbooks.com

GIRL'S BOOK·

OR

OCCUPATION FOR PLAY HOURS.

BY MISS LESLIE,

Author of Stories for Emma, the Mirror, Young Americans, Adelaide, &c.

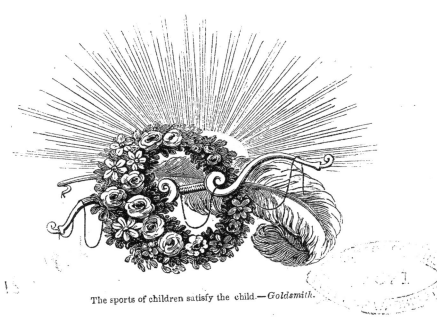

The sports of children satisfy the child.—*Goldsmith.*

BOSTON : MUNROE AND FRANCIS ;
C. S. FRANCIS, NEW-YORK.

[Entered, according to act of congress, in the Clerk's office for the District of Massachusetts, 1831, by Munroe & Francis.]

INTRODUCTION.

(SEE FRONTISPIECE.)

Henrietta, Isabella, and Juliet are seated under a tree in the garden, when they suddenly per-
ceive their mother coming to them from the house.

JULIET. Oh! here is dear mother just arrived from the city. Let us run to meet her. (*They hasten to Mrs Morrington, and she kisses them all.*)

MRS MORRINGTON. Well, my dears, I am glad to see you well, and I suppose that nothing of any consequence has happened since I left you on Wednesday ?

HENRIETTA. Nothing, mother; only that the fire-flies began to appear last evening. They were sparkling all through the garden

ISABELLA. And we heard the mocking-bird yesterday imitating the whip-poor-will, and he said those words as plainly as if he was speaking them; just like the real whip-poor-will.

O

JULIET.   And my own cantelope vine, that I planted my self, has come out with twenty-six blossoms; so I shall have a fine supply of melons.

MRS MORRINGTON.   I rejoice to hear so much good news. But I must show you a new book I have brought you, and then I will go in and take off my bonnet.

HENRIETTA.   What is it, dear mother?

MRS MORRINGTON.   It is the American Girl's Book.

ALL.   Oh! let us see it.   (*Mrs Morrington gives it to them.*)

HENRIETTA.   It is a book of recreations.   Have you read it, mother?

MRS MORRINGTON.   Yes, I read it this morning in the steam-boat.   I hope you will in future be at no loss for amusements in your play-hours.

ISABELLA.   I wish we had possessed this book before we went to Georgiana Howard's birth-day party, where nothing was thought of but playing on the piano and dancing, just as if the company were all ladies and gentlemen.

HENRIETTA.   Still I think that Georgiana Howard's party was not more dull than parties usually are—I am sure they are all equally so to me.

JULIET. And to me also ; as I have not yet began to learn music, I do not think that ugly tunes are pretty.

MRS MORRINGTON. (*smiling.*) Explain yourself.

JULIET. I mean that I do not like to sit half the evening and hear little girls playing the tiresome pieces that their teachers call " good practice." They may be very good practice, but children like me can find no meaning in them, as they seem to go all ways and with no regularity, and it is difficult to distinguish one from another.

MRS MORRINGTON. They appear so to you, because you do not understand them. I can easily imagine that to the generality of children scientific music is very fatiguing, even when well performed and by excellent musicians.

JULIET. Little girls like amusements that they can all partake of. Now when there is dancing at parties, not one half the company can get places, particularly the younger ones, so they are obliged to sit by and look on.

HENRIETTA. Besides, we have enough of music and dancing at school. That evening at Georgiana's I proposed some little plays by way of variety, but I found that no one knew any thing about that sort of amusement. I would have tried to teach them the few that I was acquainted with, but Georgiana and the elder girls persisted in dancing, and nearly all the little ones fell asleep on their chairs.

JULIET.   Are the plays and games in this book for children of all ages, dear mother ?

MRS MORRINGTON.   Yes, the first section comprises a series of sports and pastimes for little girls from four to ten years old.   Many of these amusements are designed chiefly to exercise the body, and none of them require any extraordinary effort of the mind.   These are followed by plays for girls between ten and fifteen, in most of which some degree of ingenuity is requisite.

JULIET.   But are these plays for the elder girls too difficult for the little ones ?

MRS MORRINGTON.   A few of them are.   But generally speaking, an intelligent little girl with a quick comprehension and a good memory will find any diversion in the book sufficiently easy.

HENRIETTA.   Some of the amusements in the first part of the book seem quite too childish for me.

ISABELLA.   Well, I intend to go through them all.   I think it pleasant enough to play with small children occasionally, when they are not dull or fretful, and I like to make them happy by entering into their amusements, however trifling they may appear.

MRS MORRINGTON. You see that most of these plays are not only minutely described, but also illustrated by a dialogue.

ISABELLA. The dialogues will of course enable us to comprehend the plays with more ease.

HENRIETTA. Ah! here are various ways of redeeming forfeits. In games of forfeits there is generally considerable difficulty in deciding upon what terms they are to be restored to their owners.

ISABELLA. And here are little games with cards as well as loto, domino, chequers and other similar diversions.

HENRIETTA. And here is a large collection of riddles with the answers directly under them, which will save the trouble of turning over leaves and searching out figures of reference.

ISABELLA. See—see—Here are varieties of pincushions, needle-books and reticules, with directions for making them.

JULIET. And dolls too! Here are several ways of making dolls.

MRS MORRINGTON. I will give you some pieces of silk and other materials, and you may construct as many of these articles as you please. This sort of work is not only amusing but very improving, as it teaches children expertness in cutting out and fixing, and neatness in sewing.

HENRIETTA. Juliet, I will make you a handsome linen doll exactly like this in the book.

JULIET. Thank you, Henrietta. I know I shall like it better than my wax doll, which I am always afraid to handle. I think I could myself make some of these bags and pincushions. At least I will try one or two of the easiest.

ISABELLA. I shall not fear to attempt any of them.

HENRIETTA. And I will undertake all the drawing and colouring that is to be done.

JULIET. I think I shall make a patch-work quilt for my doll.

ISABELLA. And while two of us are sewing, the other can read the riddles aloud, and we will try to guess them.

HENRIETTA. I rather think we shall know all the riddles before this sewing begins.

JULIET. Dear mother, now that you have been so kind as to bring us this book, I shall find less trouble in amusing little Marian Graham when she comes to see me. She, at least, can play "Robin's alive," and "Honey Pots," and "Bread and Cheese." She may be able also to understand some of the easiest riddles, though I doubt her guessing any of the conundrums, poor thing. And as for cutting and sewing, I dare say she could soon learn to clip the edges of the pen-wipers, or perhaps to make a black doll.

HENRIETTA. Dear mother, my birth-day will soon come. If you will permit me to have a little party, we will show how well we can get through the evening without either music or dancing, or without pretending to talk and behave like grown ladies and gentlemen. Before that time we shall have learned all these plays, and we will select for the occasion none but the most amusing, and such as the whole company can join in.

MRS MORRINGTON. I consent, my dear, willingly, and I hope your young guests will follow the example and conduct their future parties on a similar plan. Do not, however, suppose that these little plays are intended particularly for *parties*. Many of them can be just as well pursued in small families or by only two or three children.

I have often regretted that so many of the diversions which formerly enlivened the leisure hours of very young people should long since have become obsolete, or only to be found in circles which are yet untouched with the folly and affectation of what is called fashion. And also that in families where the children are *over educated* (as is now too often the case) the parents, forgetting that they themselves were once young, allow no recreations but those of so grave a character, that play becomes more difficult and fatiguing than study.

The author of this little book has not aimed at compiling a juvenile encyclopedia.—It is simply an unpretending manual of light and exhilarating amusements; most of which will be found on trial to answer the purpose of unbending the mind or exercising the body, and at the same time interesting the attention.

CONTENTS.

Part I.

SPORTS AND PASTIMES.

xii

CONTENTS.

CONTENTS. xiii

Part II.

RIDDLES.

Part III.

AMUSING WORK.—PINCUSHIONS.

VARIETIES.

AMERICAN GIRL'S BOOK.

THE

AMERICAN GIRL'S BOOK.

SPORTS AND PASTIMES.

In books, or work, or healthful play,
Let my first years be pass'd.   WATTS.

SOME of these plays requiring a more minute explanation than others, we will suppose a company of
very young girls engaged in them ; and, designating
each child by her name, we will give a short sketch,
in the dramatic or dialogue form, of what may be
said and done on the occasion, whenever we think
such an illustration will answer the purpose better
than a mere description.

1.

LADY QUEEN ANNE.

We will imagine five little girls engaged in this play, and their names may be Fanny, Lucy, Mary, Ellen, and Jane.

A ball or pincushion, or something of the kind, having been procured, Fanny leaves the room or hides her face in a corner, that she may not see what is going on, while her companions range themselves in a row, each concealing both hands under her frock or apron. The ball has been given to Ellen, but all the others must likewise keep their hands under cover, as if they had it. When all is ready, Fanny is desired to come forward, and, advancing in front of the row, she addresses any one she pleases (for instance, Lucy,) in the following words

" Lady Queen Anne, she sits in the sun,
As fair as a lily, as brown as a bun,
She sends you three letters, and prays you'll read one."

LUCY. I cannot read one, unless I read all.

FANNY. Then pray, Miss Lucy, deliver the ball.

Lucy, not being the one that has the ball, displays her empty hands ; and Fanny, finding that she has guessed wrong, retires, and comes back again as soon as she is called. She then addresses Mary in the the same words, " Lady Queen Anne," &c. ; but she is still mistaken, as Mary has not the ball. Next time Fanny accosts Ellen, and finds that she is now right ; Ellen producing the ball from under her apron. Ellen now goes out, and Fanny takes her place in the row. Sometimes the real holder of the ball happens to be the first person addressed.

2.

ROBIN'S ALIVE.

This is played by the children's sitting in a row, with a small lighted stick or a rod that burns slowly ; which had better be held with great care, that there may be no danger of setting any thing on fire. Fanny, being at the head of the row, takes the lighted stick in her hand, and blows out the flame, so that there remains only a spark, or a dull redness on the top of the stick.

Fanny then says, "Robin's alive, and alive he shall be. If he dies in my hand, my mouth shall be bridled, my back shall be saddled, and I'll be sent home to the King's whitehall." She then puts the lighted stick into the hand of Susan, who is next to her, and Susan repeats the same words, and passes it on to Lucy. After Lucy has gone through "Robin's alive," &c. she transfers the stick to the next, the fire all the time gradually fading. If it goes quite out in the hand of Mary, or any one else, Fanny must say to her, "Robin is dead, and dead he shall be. He has died in your hand, and your mouth shall be bridled, your back shall be saddled to send you home to the King's whitehall." Mary is then blindfolded, and lies down on the sofa or on the hearth-rug, with her face downwards. Each of the little girls, in turn, brings something and lays it on Mary's back; for instance, a newspaper, a book, a handkerchief, a shoe, a little basket, or any other convenient article, saying every time "Heavy, heavy what lies over you." Mary tries to guess, and when she guesses rightly she is allowed to rise. The stick is lighted again, and the play resumed. It must be remembered, that, as soon as the stick is lighted, the flame is to be blown out, so as to leave only a redness. A green rod is the best for a Robin, as it burns more slowly and lasts longer than a dry stick

If Mary guesses a book, when it is in reality a shoe, the girl who has placed it there must say, " Shoe, lie there till book comes," and so on throughout the play.

3.

THE BOOK-BINDER.

All the little girls range themselves in a row on chairs or on the sofa, each holding together the palms of her hands. Fanny, who personates the book-binder, takes a small book between her hands, and beginning at the head of the row where Lucy is seated, she taps the cover with her fingers for a moment, and then suddenly endeavours to give Lucy a smart blow with the book on her joined hands. Lucy endeavours to avoid the blow by hastily withdrawing her hands. If she is not quick enough and allows them to be struck, she must go down to the bottom or tail of the row. Fanny then proceeds to the next girl, and attempts in the same manner to strike her hands with the book ; and so on till she has got to the end of the row; after which the little girl who is then head of the line becomes book-binder.

4.

HOW MANY MILES TO BABYLON.

This is a very simple play, but is good exercise in cold weather. It is generally played by three, or five. When three only are engaged in it, one stands at each end of the room, and the third at one side; the latter is called the witch. Fanny calls out, "How many miles to Babylon?" Lucy replies, "Threescore and ten." Fanny asks, "Can I get there by candle-light?" Lucy answers, "Yes, and back again; but take care the old witch don't catch you on the road." Susan, who performs the witch, then starts forward and tries to catch one of her playmates, as they all run about in every direction to save themselves from her grasp. The one that she succeeds in catching then becomes witch, and the play proceeds as before.

If five are playing, four stand in the four corners of the room, and the fifth, who is the witch, takes the middle.

5.

HOW MANY FINGERS.

This is a very simple play, and can be understood
by children of three years old. It is played by two
only. One lays her head in the lap of the other, in
such a manner that she can see nothing. Her
companion claps her several times on the back, holding up one or more fingers saying

"Mingledy, mingledy, clap, clap,
How many fingers do I hold up?"

She must endeavour to guess. If she guesses three, when in reality only two have been held up, her play-mate says

" Three you said, and two it was,
Mingledy, mingledy, clap, clap,
How many fingers do I hold up ?" (*holding up four.*)

She guesses again, and whenever she guesses rightly, it becomes her turn to hold up her fingers, while her companion lays her head down and covers her eyes. She who holds up her fingers, changes the number every time, sometimes holding up but one, sometimes all the fingers of both hands. The thumbs must never be held up.

6.

PUSS IN THE CORNER.

This is very simple, and is played by five. One goes into each corner of the room, and the fifth stands in the middle, personating the Puss. As soon as she calls out "Poor Pussy wants a corner," they all run out of the corners to change them, and the Puss tries to get into one. She that in the scramble is left without a corner, goes into the middle as the next Puss.

7.

MR. POPE AND HIS LADY.

This may be played by any number. A small
waiter of a circular shape is provided ; or, if a round
waiter is not at hand, a little plate will do as well.
The waiter is laid on the floor in the middle of the
room. One of the company goes to it, takes it up,
and setting it on its edge gives it a vigorous twirl
with her thumb and finger, so as to make it spin
round, saying, as she takes the waiter, " By the leave

of Mr Pope and his lady" If the waiter falls with the wrong side upwards, she is to pay a forfeit; and a forfeit is also required if she forgets to say the proper words on taking it up. She then retires, and the next in turn advances and spins round the waiter, saying also " By the leave of Mr Pope and his lady."

8.

COPENHAGEN.

First procure a long piece of tape or twine, sufficient to go round the whole company, who must stand in a circle, every girl holding in each of her hands a part of the string. The last that takes her station, holds the two ends of the tape. One remains standing in the centre of the circle. She is called "the Dane," and she must endeavour to slap the hands of one of those that is holding the string, and who must try to elude the blow by hastily withdrawing her hands. If she is not sufficiently alert, and allows them to be slapped, she takes the place of the Dane, and forfeits a kiss to her. When in the middle of the ring, she in turn must try to slap the hands of some one.

9.

HONEY POTS.

A little girl sits half down on the floor, clasping her hands together under her knees. Two others, who are older and stronger, take her up by the arms and carry her round the room between them, saying, "Who'll buy a Honey Pot?" The honey pot must keep her hands tightly clasped together all the time, so as to support her knees. If she loosens them, and allows her feet to drop before she has been carried quite round the room, she is to pay a forfeit. If the company is large, several honey-pots may be carried round at once.

10.

TRACK THE RABBIT.

The girls form a circle, holding each other's hands. One, called "the Rabbit," is left out. She runs several times round the ring on the outside, and then taps one of her companions on the shoulder. She that has received the tap quits the ring and pursues the rabbit, (always following exactly in her track) the circle again joining hands. The rabbit runs round the ring and through it in every direction, passing under the arms of those in the circle, who raise them to let her pass, and her pursuer follows closely after her. As soon as she catches the rabbit, she becomes rabbit herself, and takes her place on the outside of the ring. Those in the circle must always assist the rabbit in trying to save herself from being caught.

11.

WHOOP, OR HIDE AND SEEK.

This is best played in a garden, in a farm-yard, in the woods, or in some other suitable place out of doors, where there are conveniences for hiding. The children assemble together in a group, covering their faces that they may not see, while one of them, (called the hider) conceals herself among the trees, behind the bushes, within an arbour, on the other side of a wall, under a heap of hay, or in any other place that she thinks will not be discovered. As soon as she has hidden herself, she calls out "Whoop," in a loud voice. Her companions then run about in search of her, and whoever finds her first, is the next to hide.

12.

HOT BUTTERED BEANS.

A card, a match, a scrap of ribbon, a bit of paper, or some other little thing is the article to be hidden and Fanny may be chosen to begin the play. All the other girls leave the room and stay outside of the door ; or if it is more convenient to remain in the room, they go into a corner and cover their eyes, taking care not to peep. Fanny then hides the card or whatever it may be, under the hearth-rug, beneath the table-cover, behind a window-shutter or behind the sofa, on the shelf of the piano, or in any other place she thinks proper. She then summons her play-mates by calling out, "Hot butter'd beans; please to come to supper." The other girls all run and search every where for the card. If they approach the place where it is concealed, Fanny tells them that "they burn," or that "they are warm," according to the distance. If they keep far from it she says "they are cold," or "cool." She that finds the card, hides it next time.

13.

STIR THE MUSH.

Have one chair too few, and prohibit sitting on the sofa. If seven girls are playing, allow but six chairs to remain in the room, and place them close to the wall. One of the children stands in the middle of the room, holding a stout stick, and the others walk round her, saying, "Stir the mush, stir the mush;" and she pretends to stir very hard with the stick, continuing to do so for some time.   After a while, when no one is expecting it, she knocks three times on the floor with the stick, and then drops it and joins her play-mates, who at this signal all run about and scramble for a seat.   Whoever is left without a chair, is the next to take the stick and stir the mush.

14.

TWIRL THE TRENCHER.

A plate is laid in the middle of the floor.   The leader of the play then designates all the girls by numbers, as, One, Two, Three, Four, &c. and they must take care to remember their numbers.   She then desires No. 1 to go and twirl the trencher; that is, she must take the plate between her thumb and finger and give it a hard twirl to set it spinning, at the same time calling out for No. 4, or any one she pleases.   If No. 4 does not instantly run up and catch the plate before it has done spinning round, she pays a forfeit.   If she is sufficiently alert to get to it and seize it before it falls, she must give it a twirl and make it spin, calling our for No. 2, or some one else, who must then endeavour to catch the plate in time, or pay a pawn if she fails.

15.

BREAD AND CHEESE.

This is generally played by two only. Each shuts her hands. and the closed hands are piled upon each other, Lucy's and Jane's alternately. That is, Lucy places her right hand on the table or on her knee. Then Jane puts her right hand on Lucy's. Next Lucy adds her left hand, and then Jane completes the pile by putting her left hand on the top of Lucy's. When the hands are arranged, Lucy (whose hand

2

is undermost) asks Jane, " What have you there ?"
Jane replies, " Bread and cheese." Lucy tells her to
" eat it up;" which Jane pretends to do by withdrawing her left hand and putting it to her mouth ;
as if eating her bread and cheese. Jane then asks
Lucy " what she has there ?" and Lucy replies in the
same manner. Lucy then puts the question to Jane,
who after taking away her right hand commences
the following dialogue, while Lucy (till it is over)
continues to keep her right hand closed and resting
on the table.

JANE. What have you there ?
LUCY. A chest.
JANE. What is in it ?
LUCY. Bread and cheese.
JANE. Where is my share ?
LUCY. The cat has got it.
JANE. Where is the cat ?
LUCY. In the woods.
JANE. Where are the woods ?
LUCY. Fire has burned them.
JANE. Where is the fire ?
LUCY. Water has quenched it.
JANE. Where is the water ?
LUCY. The ox has drank it.
JANE. Where is the ox ?
LUCY. The butcher has killed him.

JANE. Where is the butcher ?

LUCY. Behind the door cracking nuts ; and whoever speaks the first word shall have three twitches by the ear and three squeezes by the hand.

They then try which can remain silent the longest. If either speaks, the other twitches her ear and squeezes her hand three times. If the play is repeated, it is Jane's turn to have her hand at the bottom and to answer the questions.

16.

FROG IN THE MIDDLE.

She that personates the Frog stands in the middle of the room, and her companions run round her saying, " Frog in the middle, you can't catch me." Now and then the Frog suddenly jumps out and endeavours to seize on one of her playmates, who if caught becomes Frog and takes her station in the centre. The Frog, when she jumps out of the middle, must not pursue or run after any one, but must try to catch by a sudden spring and grasp.

17.

THE CHRISTMAS BAG.

Fill with sugar plums a large bag of thin white paper and tie a string round the top to keep it fast.

Then suspend it to the centre of a large door-frame (the folding door for instance), or to the ceiling if convenient. Each of the children must be blindfolded in turn, and provided with a long stick. They are then led within reach of the bag and directed to try while blindfolded to strike the bag with the stick, and are allowed to make three attempts ; after which, if unsuccessful, they must give place to the next. The play goes on in this manner till some one strikes the bag with the stick so as to tear a hole in the paper ; upon which the sugar plums fall out and are scattered over the floor, when all the children scramble for them. For older children there may be a second bag filled with little books, small pin-cushions, bodkins, emery-bags, ribbon-yards, and things of a similar description.

This amusement may be concluded, by one of the family bringing in a bag which has been secretly filled with flour, and hanging it to the door frame as if, like the others, it was stored with sugar plums or pretty things. The company must not be apprized of its real contents, and must as before try blindfolded to strike it with the stick. When a hole is torn in the bag, every one near it will be dusted with the flour.

18.

OF WHAT TRADE IS OUR FAVOURITE?

Lucy goes out while her play-mates decide on a trade, Fanny having previously taken her aside and whispered to her that the trade fixed on, will be the one mentioned immediately after a profession. The other girls are not to know that this is the manner in which Lucy will be enabled to guess. After Lucy has retired, they fix on a trade, which may be that of a grocer, for instance. When Lucy is called in, Fanny asks her "of what trade is our favourite ?"

LUCY.   You must question me farther.
FANNY.   Is he a silversmith ?
LUCY.   No.
FANNY.   Is he the jeweller across the street ?
LUCY.   No.
FANNY.   Is he the bookseller at the corner ?
LUCY.   No.
FANNY.   Is he the cabinet-maker in the next street ?
LUCY.   No.
FANNY.   Is he the doctor that attends your family ?
LUCY.   No.
FANNY.   Is he the grocer that sells such good tea ?
LUCY.   Yes.
ALL.   It is a grocer. How could Lucy guess so rightly ?

The girls are not aware that Lucy knew she might say "yes" to Fanny's next question after naming the doctor or professional man ; law, physic, and divinity being called professions.

Mary goes out next, Fanny having first whispered to her that she would ask her the right question immediately after mentioning a lawyer. The trade fixed on for the favourite is watch-maker, and Mary of course guesses rightly after hearing a professional man named.

There is a similar play called Four Legs, in which any word may be fixed on, such as hat, shovel, fish, bonnet, &c. The word, which is mentioned immediately before the right one, must be something that has four legs; as, dog, horse, table, sofa, chair, &c. When, for instance, the guesser having been previously asked a variety of words, hears the question " Is it a cat ?" she may safely reply " yes" to the next question ; a cat having four legs.

THE KING AND HIS TRAIN.

19.

THE KING AND HIS TRAIN.

Two of the tallest girls (who perform the warders as they are called) go into the middle of the room, and each takes a name, whispering the name to each other so as not to be heard by the rest. The names may be gold, silver, diamonds, pearl, lily, tulip, or any thing they please. The other children then range themselves in procession, each holding the skirt of the one directly before her. The two warders that stand in the centre of the room take each other's hands, and raise their arms as high as possible, calling out, as the procession passes under,

" We'll open the gates as high as the sky
And let the king and his train pass by,"

and trying to catch one of the little girls by putting their joined arms suddenly down, so as to encircle her neck. The little girls must try to avoid this by stooping their heads as they pass under the arms. When one is caught, the two warders ask her in a whisper whether she chooses gold or silver, or a pearl or a diamond, according to the names they have taken. If she chooses gold, she goes behind the warder of that name, and stands there till the play is over, holding by her frock. Should she choose the other, she goes behind silver. The warders then raise their arms again, holding each other's hands, and the rhyme " We'll open the gates," &c. is repeated as before. The play goes on in this manner till the king and all his train are caught, and put behind one or other of the warders. After this, two girls of the next size become warders.

Of those that form the procession the tallest is always king, and the others take their places according to height, the smallest walking last.

The procession walks round the warders every time previous to passing under their arms.

20.

SEWING SCHOOL.

The girls sit down in a row, each taking a portion of her apron or frock and holding it up in both hands between her thumb and forefinger. One who represents the mistress of the sewing-school, goes along the row and says to each one something about her sewing, endeavouring to engage the attention of the sewer while she (the mistress) takes an opportunity of striking it suddenly out of her hands. If the sewer is off her guard and allows her sewing to be struck down, she pays a forfeit. For instance. Suppose all the girls seated in a row, and holding their aprons so as to represent sewing. Fanny goes along, stopping at each and saying, "Lucy, have you come to the seam yet ? Mary, you are puckering your work. Anne, your stitches are too long. Ellen, you don't fasten off well. Jane, your thread is going to break. Rosa, your hem is crooked. Ah ! I have struck it out of your hand. You should have held it fast. So now give me something for a forfeit."

21.

THE BLIND POINTER.

One that performs the Pointer is blindfolded and stands in the middle of the room holding a long stick in her hand. The others go round, each as she passes making some noise, such as laughing, crying, coughing, sneezing, clapping her hands, or stamping her feet. The pointer must endeavour to guess who she is by the noise, pointing the stick towards her and calling our her name. Whoever is guessed rightly becomes Pointer.

22.

THE HEN AND CHICKENS.

One of the girls who personates a Fox takes her seat on the floor in the middle of the room. The others, having the eldest at the head, form a procession holding each other's skirts in both hands, and walk round the Fox, the foremost girl who performs the Hen saying

> "Chickany chickany craney crow,
> I went to the well to wash my toe,
> And when I came back a chicken was dead."

The next girl repeats the same rhyme; and so on till each has said it in her turn. Then they all stop near the fox, and the hen says "What are you doing, old fox?"

Fox. Making a fire.
HEN. What for ?
Fox. To heat some water.
HEN. For what is the water ?
Fox. To scald a chicken.
HEN. Where will you get it ?
Fox. Out of your flock.

At these words the fox starts up, and the hen and chickens disperse and run away in every direction. The fox pursues them, and when she succeeds in catching a chicken, that chicken becomes fox, and seats herself in the middle of the room; while the former fox takes the place of the hen at the head of the procession of chickens.

23.

HUNT THE SLIPPER.

The girls seat themselves on the floor in a circle in the middle of the room, all except one who remains out, as the hunter, and stands in the centre of the ring. A shoe or slipper is then taken off, and they shove it about secretly from one to another, passing it behind their feet and behind their backs, and in any way that will prevent the hunter from seeing it. The hunter's object is to detect and snatch away the slipper while the girls are privately conveying it round the circle, and *their* aim is to prevent her from seeing it or from knowing who has it; though the possessor frequently knocks on the floor with it, when the hunter is not looking towards her. As soon as the hunter gets hold of the slipper, she takes a seat in the circle, and the one with whom she has happened to find the slipper then becomes hunter.

24.

THE THIMBLE.

The company sit in a row holding together the palms of their hands. Fanny takes a thimble or any thing else that is small and round, (for instance, a hazel-nut or a shell-bark) and holding it between her palms, she goes along the line, pretending to drop it secretly into their hands, saying to each "Hold fast what I give you." Every one opens her hands as if she was receiving the thimble, and closes them again immediately. Of course the thimble is only in reality deposited with one. For instance, Fanny leaves it in the hands of Lucy.

After Fanny has in this manner gone all along the row, she returns to the head and asks Mary, who is seated there, to guess who has the thimble. Mary guesses Jane, who opens her hands and shows that she has it not. They all guess in turn. Susan happens to guess Lucy ; and this being right, Lucy displays the thimble and gives it to Susan. It is then Susan's turn to take the thimble and go along the row with it.

Sometimes when this is played, a forfeit is required from every one that guesses wrong, and therefore a great number of pawns are speedily collected.

25.

THE TEN FINE BIRDS.

The company sit in a circle, and the play begins by one of the girls saying, " A good fat hen ;" this is repeated by the whole circle in turn, but only one must speak at a time. When all have said, " A good fat hen," the leader of the play begins again and gives out, " Two ducks and a good fat hen ;" which is also repeated separately by the whole company.

The next is, " Three squawking wild geese, two ducks and a good fat hen." After this has gone round as before the leader says, "Four plump partridges, three squawking wild geese, two ducks, and a good fat hen." This having been repeated by all, the next that is given out is, "Five pouting pigeons, four plump partridges, three squawking wild geese, two ducks, and a good fat hen." Afterwards, "Six long-legged cranes, five pouting pigeons, four plump partridges, three squawking wild geese, two ducks, and a good fat hen." Next, "Seven green parrots, six long-legged cranes, five pouting pigeons, four plump partridges, three squawking wild geese, two ducks, and a good fat hen." Next, "Eight screeching owls, seven green parrots, six long-legged cranes, five pouting pigeons, four plump partridges, three squawking wild geese, two ducks, and a good fat hen." Next, "Nine ugly turkey-buzzards, eight screeching owls, seven green parrots, six long-legged cranes, five pouting pigeons, four plump partridges, three squawking wild geese, two ducks, and a good fat hen." Lastly, "Ten bald eagles, nine ugly turkey-buzzards, eight screeching owls, seven green parrots, six long-legged cranes, five pouting pigeons, four plump partridges, three squaking wild geese, two ducks, and a good fat hen."

All this must go round the whole company every time, and be repeated separately by each. If any one hesitates or leaves out any thing, or makes a mistake, she must pay a forfeit.

The House that Jack built, (which is well known to all children) may be converted into a similar play; each of the company first repeating separately "This is the House that Jack built;" and so on till they have got through the whole, adding more every time it goes round, and paying a pawn for every omission or error.

26.

KING AND QUEEN.

The company sit in two rows, facing each other. There must be an even number, as six, eight, ten or twelve. One row personates a range of gentlemen with a king sitting at the end. The opposite row is to consist of ladies, she at the head being queen.

3

The king numbers all the gentlemen, 1, 2, 3, &c. and they must remember their numbers. The queen numbers the ladies, but all their numbers must be different from those of the gentlemen. For instance, if the gentlemen are 1, 2, 3, 4, 5, the ladies must be 6, 7, 8, 9, 10.

When all is arranged, the king and queen each call out a number. If the king calls No. 2, he who bears that title must start up and run all round the company. The queen must at the same time call out one of her ladies; for instance No. 8, and the lady must pursue the gentleman all round. If she catches him before he gets to the king, he pays a forfeit. They then resume their seats, and it is the queen's turn to call first. She may call No. 10, and the king No. 4. The gentleman now pursues the lady, and if he catches her before she gets to the queen, she pays a forfeit.

Sometimes in this play, all the odd numbers as 1, 3, 5, 7, are allotted to the gentlemen, and the even numbers, 2, 4, 6, 8, are given to the ladies.

27.

THE DUTCH DOLL.

All the company go out of the room, except two who are well acquainted with the play; the others had better be ignorant of it. We will suppose that Fanny and Lucy are left together to prepare the doll, which doll is to be performed by Fanny. For this purpose she lies at full length under a table covered with a deep cloth, or that has large leaves descending nearly to the floor. Her face must be downwards. Lucy, having previously procured the necessary articles, dresses Fanny's feet with a frock or petti-

coat, adding a cloak or shawl and an old bonnet
or hood, pinning and tying on the things so as to
look something like a large and very dowdy doll.
The company are then called in, and if they have
not seen a Dutch doll before, are at a loss to conceive
what it can be. Before they come in, Fanny must
raise her feet so that the doll appears to stand upright; and as soon as they enter she must begin
to kick her feet up and down and shuffle them about
in such a way as to make the doll seem to dance and
jump and bow, and play all sorts of antics, frequently
seeming to knock her forehead against the floor. If
the doll is well performed, it is very laughable, and if
Fanny takes care to be well concealed under the
table, no one unacquainted with the play can guess
that it is set in motion by her feet. She must be sure
to lie on her face.

If a boy is in company, he should be made to personate the doll.

28.

FARMERS AND MECHANICS.

One leaves the room while the others fix on a
trade, which when she returns they must all endeav-

our to represent by their actions, so that she can guess for what they intend themselves. When she guesses, the next in size or age goes out, and her companions try something else. If, on coming in, she finds all her play-mates with chairs turned down which they push before them as if ploughing, or if they are tossing about their handkerchiefs with sticks as if making hay, she rightly guesses them to be farmers. If they are sitting on low seats and mending their shoes, she knows them to be cobblers, or if they are seated on the tables cross-legged and sewing, they are meant for tailors. They may pretend to be sawing and planing like carpenters, hammering iron on anvils or shoeing horses like blacksmiths, spreading mortar with trowels and climbing ladders like brick-layers building a house, &c. They may, if they choose, all work at different parts of the same trade, provided always that every one is a farmer, a cobbler, a tailor, or whatever trade they have chosen for the whole.

Ingenious children can make this play very amusing.

29.

SHE CAN DO LITTLE WHO CAN'T DO THIS.

One who understands the play takes the tongs and holds them in both hands, putting one hand on the head or knob of the tongs, and the other on one of the legs. She must knock the points of the tongs three times on the floor, saying, " She can do little who can't do this." She then transfers them to her next neighbour, who, if unacquainted with the play, will not hold the tongs in the right way, and in both hands ; thinking that it is only necessary to knock on the floor with them and repeat the words. If she holds them wrong, she pays a forfeit, and in this way the tongs must be handed round to the whole company ; each repeating the words, and knocking three times on the floor. If none do right, the proper way is not to be explained till the play is over, that the more pawns may be collected.

If any one knows the play and does it rightly, she must not tell the others, till all have tried it.

Simple as this play is, very few, who are not familiar with it, will chance to hold the tongs in the proper manner.

.30.

BLINDMAN'S BUFF.

One of the company must be blindfolded with a handkerchief, tied round her eyes in such a manner that she cannot possibly see. She is then led into the middle of the room, and a rhyme is repeated while her companions are retiring from her reach. She then goes about the room endeavouring to catch somebody, and her playmates try their utmost to keep out of her way. No one, however, must leave the room, and no one must mischievously annoy the blind-girl by pinching, pulling, or in any way teazing her. If she approaches any thing that may hurt her, (the fire, for instance,) her companions must immediately call out to apprize her of her danger. It is better, before the play begins, to take up and lay aside the hearth-rug, lest some one should catch her foot in it and fall. The fender also should be turned up on its two ends, as a sort of guard against the fire. When the blind-girl catches any one, she must endeavour to guess who it is, for which purpose she is allowed to pass her hands over the head and dress of her captive. If she cannot guess, she must let the prisoner go, and try to catch some one else. The first girl that is caught, and guessed rightly, is the next to be blindfolded.

Example.

FANNY. Well, Lucy, are you ready to be blindfolded ? *(Fanny ties a handkerchief round Lucy's eyes.)* There now. Are you sure you do not see ?

LUCY. I never cheat when I play.

FANNY. I know you are very honourable. But when Sarah Granby plays blindman's buff, she always manages to slip up the bandage, in such a way, that she can see all the time, and catch whoever she pleases. There now, give me your hand. *(She leads Lucy into the middle of the room.)*

How many horses are in your father's stable ?

Lucy. Three.

Fanny. Of what colours are they ?

Lucy. Black, white, and grey.

Fanny. Turn round three times and catch who you may.

(Lucy extends her hands, and turns round three times, the girls all taking care to be out of her reach. She then gropes about for some time, and catches no one. Once she gets the skirts of Rosa's frock between her thumb and finger, but her hold being very slight, Rosa easily disengages herself and makes her escape. Lucy then catches Ellen by the end of her sash, and Ellen gets away by untying the sash, and leaving it in Lucy's hand.)

Lucy. I have somebody now. Why, no—I believe it is only a ribbon. Ah ! there has been some trick.

Jane. *(In a low voice.)* Ellen, is this quite fair ?

Fanny. No, indeed it is not. However, we will pass it over. I know, Lucy likes to be blindfolded.

Jane. That's more than I do. When I am blinded, I am afraid to move a step. But I see that Lucy rambles about quite briskly, notwithstanding the bandage over her eyes.

Fanny. Hush ! she will distinguish you by your voice. *(Mary slips into a closet.)* Now, Mary, come out of the closet. That really is not fair.

Lucy. Ah ! I hear a cluster of you laughing in yon corner. I will be among you in a moment.

(Lucy goes to a corner where several of the girls have retreated, and catches Isabel by the arm. The others, having crouched down, slip away, creeping along the floor.)

Fanny. Well, Lucy ! who have you there ?

Lucy. It is Mary. I know her by the stiffening in her sleeves.

(They all laugh and exclaim, " Oh, no ! no !")

Fanny. You are mistaken ; it is Isabel : she also has stiffened sleeves. You must let her go, and try to catch some one else. *(Lucy releases Isabel, and goes about in quest of another. Anne hides behind the window curtain.)*

LUCY. Ah! I am near the window. I feel the fringe of the curtain. And some one is hidden behind it. *(She presses the curtain closely around Anne, who laughs.)* That is Anne's laugh. I have caught her in a trap. Come out, Miss Anne. It is your turn now.

(She takes off the handkerchief, and blindfolds Anne.)

31.

THE BELLS OF LONDON.

This should be played in a field, or in some place where there is no danger of being hurt by falling.

The two tallest of the company join their hands and raise them high above their heads, while the others, (each holding the skirt of the one before her,) walk under in procession, as in the King and his Train. The two, that are holding up their hands, sing the following rhymes :—

" Oranges and lemons,
  Say the bells of St Clements ;
  Brickdust and tiles,
  Say the bells of St Giles ;
  You owe me five farthings,
  Say the bells of St Martin's ;

When will you pay me ?
Say the bells of Old Bailey ;
When I grow rich,
Say the bells of Shoreditch ;
When will that be ?
Say the bells of Stepney ;
I do not know,
Says the great bell of Bow."

At the last line, they suddenly lower their arms and endeavour to catch one of those that is passing under. Having each previously fixed on a name, (for instance, one Nutmeg, the other, Cinnamon,) they ask their captive which she chooses, Nutmeg or Cinnamon. Accordingly as she answers, she is put behind one or the other. When all have been caught and placed behind, those at each end join hands, so as to encircle the two in the middle; and they must wind round them till they get closer and closer. The rhyme "Oranges and lemons," &c. is then repeated ; and at the words "Great bell of Bow," those in the centre must give a sudden push and extricate themselves by throwing down all the rest.

THE PRUSSIAN EXERCISE.

32.

THE PRUSSIAN EXERCISE.

All the children kneel down in a row, except one who personates the captain, and who ought to be a smart girl and well acquainted with the play, which is more diverting when all the others are ignorant of it, except the one at the head of the line. If the corporal, as this one is called, does not know the play, the captain must take her aside and inform her of the manner of concluding it.

When all are ready, the captain stands in front of the line and gives the word of command, telling them always to do something that has a diverting or ludicrous effect, when done by the whole company at the same moment. For instance : the captain gives the word to cough, and they must all cough as loudly as possible. They may be ordered to pull their own hair ; to pull their own noses ; to slap their own cheeks ; to clap their hands together ; to laugh ; to wink their eyes ; or do any other ridiculous thing. All. however, must be done at once, and by the whole line, the corporal setting the example.

Finally, the captain orders them to " Present."
Each then projects forward one arm, holding it out
straight before her. The next command is to " Fire."
Upon which the corporal gives her next neighbour a
sudden push, which causes her to fall against the next,
and in this manner the whole line is thrown down
sideways, one tumbling on another.

This is rather a boisterous play, but it can be made
very laughable ; and there need be no fear of the
children getting hurt in falling, if they play on the
grass, or in a hay-field, or if they take the precaution
of laying cushions, pillows, or something soft, at the
end of the line to receive the one that falls last ;
she being in the most danger.

There are few of these diversions that will not end
in hurts and disasters if played rudely and mischievously. But, if conducted with proper discretion,
no objection need be made to them.

33.

DRESSING THE LADY.

First decide that a certain colour shall not be mentioned, under penalty of a forfeit ; for instance, you

may interdict either green, blue, yellow, or pink. One asks, " How shall my lady be dressed for the ball ?" Each in turn proposes an article of dress ; if any one mentions the forbidden colour, she must pay a forfeit. When the dress of the lady is completed, the pawns or forfeits must be sold. Sometimes two colours are prohibited.

Example.

FANNY. What colour shall we avoid mentioning ?

LUCY. Black.

FANNY. Let us forbid white also. We shall collect the more forfeits if two colours are excluded. Therefore let no one mention either black or white. How shall my lady be drest for the ball ?

LUCY. She shall have a yellow silk frock.

MARY. With green satin trimming.

LYDIA. Pearl necklace and bracelets.

SUSAN. White satin shoes.

FANNY. Ah! a forfeit already. You should not have said, *white* satin.

SUSAN. Oh! why did not I think of *black* satin shoes ?

FANNY. That would have been as bad. You forget that black is prohibited, as well as white.

SUSAN. Well, take these scissors as a forfeit. Come, let the play go on.

JANE. My lady shall have a blue gauze scarf.

ANNE. Pink ribbon to loop up her sleeves.

ELLEN. White kid gloves. Long gloves.

FANNY. *White* kid. A forfeit again.

ELLEN. But nobody wears coloured gloves at a ball.

FANNY. Then you need not have mentioned the gloves.

ELLEN. This card will do for a forfeit.

ISABEL. My lady shall have scarlet flowers in her hair.

FANNY. What a variety of colours ! She will look like a great bunch of flowers.

CATHERINE. A purple velvet reticule.

ROSA. A black velvet belt.

FANNY. Black velvet—*black*—a forfeit, Rosa.

ROSA. But no other velvet would look so well for a belt as black.

FANNY. No matter ; you should have said something else. Where is your forfeit ?

ROSA. Take this chestnut.

FANNY. Well, I believe my lady is sufficiently drest ; so, Lucy, the play may go round again, and you may dress yours.

LUCY. This time the forbidden colours shall be blue and green. So " how shall my lady be drest for the ball ?"

34.

THE THRONE OF COMPLIMENTS.

The girls take it in turn to be the Lady Fair, beginning with the tallest, who takes her seat on a chair at the upper end of the room. The others all remain at the lower end in a row, except one who stands in the middle of the apartment and is called the Judge. When all are ready, every one makes a low curtsy to the lady, and the judge says ·

" The Lady Fair sits like a queen on her throne,
Give her your praises, and let her alone."

Each of the girls in turn goes up to the judge, and whispers something in praise of the lady, taking care to remember what it is. When the compliments have all been paid, the judge repeats them aloud, one at a time, and the Lady Fair endeavours to guess the author of each compliment, and the judge tells her whether she is right or wrong. Whenever the Lady guesses wrong, she pays a forfeit, all of which she is to redeem before another takes the throne. The most accurate way of recollecting the compliments is for the judge to have a slate, and write them all down as she hears them.

Example.

Lucy. Fanny, you are the tallest, so you must be our first Lady Fair ; and, as I am the next in height, I will be Judge. Come, girls, range yourselves in a row at the bottom of the room, while I stand in the middle with my slate, and Fanny takes her seat at the upper end. Are you all ready ? Then let us make our curtsies. (*They curtsy to Fanny.*)

"The Lady Fair sits like a queen on her throne,
Give her your praises, and let her alone"

(*The girls go up one at a time to Lucy, and whisper to her something in compliment to Fanny, which the judge writes down on her slate.*)

Well, have you all paid your compliments ? Then I will read them to the Lady Fair. (*She reads.*)

4

Somebody says, the Lady Fair is very good-tempered.

FANNY. That was Susan.

LUCY. No, it was Lydia : So, a forfeit from your ladyship.

FANNY. As the forfeits will be all mine, and as I expect to have many, I will give for each forfeit a flower from this nosegay. So here is a rose-bud. Now go on.

LUCY. Some one said, the Lady Fair has very bright eyes.

FANNY. That was Jane.

LUCY. No, it was Isabel. So, another forfeit. Some one says, the Lady Fair has beautiful ringlets.

FANNY. That was Catherine.

LUCY. Yes, it *was* Catherine. Some one says, the Lady Fair sings very well.

FANNY. Rosa said that.

LUCY. No; Susan said it. So, a forfeit. Somebody says, the Lady Fair dances gracefully.

FANNY. That was Mary.

LUCY. No—it was Ellen. A forfeit again. Some one said, the Lady Fair always minds her stops when she reads aloud.

FANNY. That must be Jane.

LUCY. No ; it was Rosa. So a forfeit again. Somebody said, the Lady Fair takes short stitches when she sews.

FANNY. Anne must have said that.

LUCY. You are right this time ; it *was* Anne. Some one said, the Lady Fair is clever at all sorts of plays.

FANNY. That was Mary.

LUCY. No, it was myself. "That is the compliment that I have written at the close of the list. But, as you guessed wrong, one more forfeit. You have now six pawns to redeem. When that is done, I shall have the honour of being Lady Fair, and Susan will perform the Judge.

35.

THE APPRENTICE.

She that begins the play says, that she apprenticed her son to a tailor, shoemaker, grocer, or any other mechanic or tradesman, and she mentions the initial letters only of the first article he made or sold. The other girls endeavour to guess her meaning. If all are unable to discover it, and therefore give it up, she again apprentices her son. Whoever guesses rightly, takes her turn. This can be played by two only, or by any number.

Example.

FANNY. I apprenticed my son to a grocer, and the first thing he sold was C.

MARY. Coffee—coffee

FANNY. No ; I did not mean coffee.

JANE. Chocolate.

FANNY. Right. Now it is your turn.

JANE. I apprenticed my son to a confectioner, and the first thing he sold was M. S.

LUCY. Oh ! Mint-stick—mint-stick. Well, I also apprenticed my son to a confectioner, and the first things he sold were B. A.

ALL. B. A. We never can guess B. A.

LUCY. Try.

ELLEN. Oh ! Burnt Almonds. I apprenticed my son to a cake-baker, and the first things he made were G. N.

Lucy. G. N. What can G. N. be ? *(They all ponder awhile, and at last agree to give it up.)*

Ellen. Gingerbread-nuts.

Mary. Oh! why did not I think of them, when I like them so much ? You again, Ellen.

Ellen. I apprenticed my son to a gardener, and the first root he planted was a T.

Mary. A tulip.

Ellen. Yes; a tulip.

Mary. I apprenticed my son to an iron-monger, and the first thing he sold was a F. P.

Jane. A frying-pan.——I apprenticed my son to a cabinet-maker, and the first thing he made was a C. T.

Fanny. A Centre-Table. I apprenticed my son to a stationer, and the first thing he sold was S. W.

Ellen. Sealing-Wax. I apprenticed my son to a stationer, and the first thing he sold was an A.

Mary. An A—An A. I give it up.

All. *(after a pause.)* We all give it up.

Ellen. An Almanack.

Mary. I thought only booksellers sold almanacks.

Ellen. And stationers also. When I go into a store, I always look round attentively, and try to remember every thing I see there.

36.

THE TRAVELLER.

One personates the Traveller, others take the names of Landlord, Landlady, Chambermaid, Waiter, Ostler, and Boot-cleaner, and the rest are denominated Horse, Saddle, Bridle, Oats, Boots, Slippers, Supper,

Candle, Bed, &c. ; all the names having reference to an inn or tavern, and to the probable wants of a traveller.

When all the others are seated round the room, the Traveller comes in, and says, " Landlady, can I have supper and a bed here to-night ?" Upon this, Landlady, Supper, and Bed all start up together. The Traveller may then say, " Landlord, I want a bottle of cider and the newspaper." If any are named Cider and Newspaper, they must start up with the Landlord. The Traveller then calls the ostler, to take the saddle and bridle off his horse, and feed him with oats. Upon which Ostler, Horse, Saddle, Bridle, and Oats, all start up as soon as they hear their names. The Traveller then desires the waiter to bring him his supper, and then Waiter and Supper respond. Lastly, he calls the chambermaid to bring him a candle, and the boot-boy to bring him slippers and take his boots ; upon which, Chambermaid, Candle, Boot-boy, Slippers, and Boots, all rise. If any one omits getting up, when her name is mentioned by the Traveller, she pays a forfeit.

With a smart Traveller, this play may be made very amusing. Any thing may be said that brings in the names of the com   .

MAGICAL MUSIC.

37:

MAGICAL MUSIC.

One of the company leaves the room, and the others fix on something to be done by her when she returns, such as looking in the glass, snuffing the candle, sweeping the hearth, pouring out and drinking a glass of water, reading a book, &c. After they have come to a decision, she is called in, and tries to discover her allotted task by attempting whatever she thinks most probable. In the mean time, one of her companions is seated at the piano, and strikes a key slowly as long as the experiments are going wrong. When they seem likely to succeed, she touches the key more rapidly ; and when exactly right, she strikes as fast as possible. If there is no piano in the room, a handbell rung slowly or rapidly will do as well, or the striking of a large door-key against the tongs or shovel may be substituted.

Example.

Maria, Julia, Sophia, Harriet, Louisa, Helen, and several others, all seated in a row, and arranged according to their size.

MARIA. Harriet, as you are the tallest, you must go out first, and wait in the entry till we have decided on something for you to do. Shut the door very tightly, Harriet, and be sure not to listen.

HARRIET. Can you suppose I would be guilty of any thing so dis-honourable ?   *(She goes out.)*

MARIA. Now what shall be her task ?

LOUISA. Let her take up a book, and read in it.

HELEN. Let her raise the sash, and look out of the window.

SOPHIA. Let her go to the side-board, pour out a glass of water, and drink some of it.

MARIA. Yes, that will do very well. Julia, do you sit down to the piano.

(Julia takes her seat at the instrument, and Maria goes to the door and calls in Harriet, who immediately approaches the looking-glass to survey herself. This not being right, Harriet touches the piano very slowly. Harriet then goes to the table and takes up a book; the piano is still slow. She then attempts to look out of the window; the piano continues slow. Next, she goes towards the side-board, and Julia strikes the piano a little faster. Harriet takes up the water-pitcher, and the piano goes faster still. She pours some water into a glass, and the piano is still faster; she drinks the water, and the piano goes as fast as possible, the girls exclaiming, " That's right, that's right."

MARIA. Sophia, you are next.   *(Sophia goes out.)*

HELEN. Let Sophia's task be to play a little on the piano.

MARIA. Excellent. It will be a long time before she thinks of that. *(Opening the door.)* Come in, Sophia.

(Sophia sweeps the hearth, snuffs the candles, removes the cushion from the sofa, piles one stool on another, opens a work-basket and begins to sew, dances a few steps, and attempts several other things, the piano all the time going slowly. At last, the right thought happens suddenly to enter her head. She approaches the piano, and Julia touches it faster. Sophia then goes behind Julia, who is seated on the music-stool, and stretching out her arms over Julia's shoulders, she plays with both hands a few

lines of a popular song, singing the air ; Julia all the time
touching the piano as fast as she can, but very softly.)

MARIA. Well, Sophia, you have guessed it at last. I was afraid,
for awhile, you would be obliged to give it up in despair.

38.

CHITTERBOB.

The company are to sit in a row, and the following is to be · repeated by each in turn, without the
slightest variation or mistake.

> There was a man and his name was Cob,
> He had a wife and her ‾name was Mob,
> He had a dog and his name was Bob,
> She had a cat and her name was Chitterbob.
>   " Bob," says Cob ;
>   " Chitterbob," says Mob.
> Bob was Cob's dog ;
> Chitterbob was Mob's cat—
>   Cob, Mob, Bob and Chitterbob.

If, in reciting the above lines, any mistake is made,
however slight, the delinquent is to have a long piece
of paper twisted into her front hair in such a manner
as to stand out and resemble a horn.   If the play goes
round several times, it is probable that most of the
players will have three or four horns on their heads.

Some paper should be previously prepared.

These horns answer the same purpose as pawns or forfeits, and are to be taken off one by one when redeemed. The pawn-seller is as usual to be blindfolded, and the crier of the pawns is to touch one of the horns, and say, "How shall this lady get rid of her horn?" The pawn-seller then proposes one of the customary methods.

39.

HOW DO YOU LIKE IT?

One leaves the room, while the others fix on a word that has two or more meanings, as sash (of a window, or of silk,) corn a sort of grain, and corn on the toe, &c. The absentee is then called in, and goes round the company inquiring of each, "How do you like it?" All the replies must be in reference to the signification of the word in one or other of its meanings. She, whose answer causes it to be rightly guessed, is the next to go out.

Example.

MARIA. Well, now we have sent Julia into the entry, what word shall we fix on?

LOUISA. Box—*that* has several meanings : box, a chest ; box at the theatre ; box, a garden plant.

MARIA. Right. Box it shall be. Come in, Julia. *(Julia comes in, and addresses Maria.)*

JULIA. Well, Maria, how do you like it ?

MARIA. I like it of red morocco.

JULIA. How do you like it, Helen ?

HELEN. I like it green and flourishing.

JULIA. And you, Louisa ?

LOUISA. I like it front and not crowded.

JULIA. Of red morocco—green and flourishing—front, and no crowded—what can it be ! Well, Sophia ?

SOPHIA. Of painted velvet.

JULIA. How do you like it, Emily ?

EMILY. Filled with agreeable people, who are attentive to what they see.

JULIA. Of painted velvet—filled with agreeable people—I am more puzzled than ever. Well, Caroline, how do *you* like it ?

CAROLINE. Full of sugar-plums.

JULIA. Ah ! I know what it is—a box—a box—I wonder I was so long guessing.

MARIA. Come, Caroline, you must go out, as Julia took the idea from your answer.

CAROLINE. Do not give me any thing that is very difficult. *(She goes out.)*

MARIA. What word shall we have for her ?

JULIA. As Caroline is the youngest among us, we will, as she says, give her something easy.

SOPHIA. Lock—lock, a fastening—a lock of hair.

MARIA. That will do. Come in, Caroline. *(Caroline returns.)*

CAROLINE. How do you like it, Maria ?

MARIA. Of brass.

CAROLINE. Well, Helen ?

HELEN. Soft and silky.

CAROLINE. Of brass—soft and silky—how can it be both ! Now, Louisa ?

LOUISA. Of jet-black.

CAROLINE. Well, Sophia ?

SOPHIA. I like it with a cut-glass handle ?

CAROLINE. What can it be ? How do you like it, Emily.

EMILY. Curled in ringlets.

CAROLINE. It must then be hair. And yet of brass, and with a glass handle—Oh ! a lock, a lock.

EMILY. You are right. As you guessed it from me, I will go out.

40.

WHAT IS MY THOUGHT LIKE ?

The company having taken their places, the one at the head of the row thinks of a word ; for instance, the sun, the river, a bonnet, a frock, and asks the others " what her thought is like ?" The first reply is made by the one next to the thinker, and so on till each has in turn given an answer. As none of them know the thought, the reply is of course always at random, and may be " like a pin," " like a glove," " like the wind," &c. The thinker must remember by whom each answer was given ; and when all have made their replies, she proclaims her thought, and each must give a reason why her answer resembles the thought.   Whoever is unable to find a reason must pay a forfeit.   Afterwards it is the turn of the one next to the head to have a thought.

Example.

MARIA.   Julia, what is my thought like ?
JULIA.   Like rain.
MARIA.   Louisa, what do you say ?
LOUISA.   Like a flower.
MARIA.   Well, Charlotte ?
CHARLOTTE.   Like a bell.
MARIA.   Sophia, you are next.
SOPHIA.   Like an owl.
MARIA.   Come, Helen ?
HELEN.   Like a star.
MARIA.   And now Emily.
EMILY.   Like a cheese.
MARIA.   Rain—a flower—a bell—an owl—a star—a cheese.
JULIA.   I cannot imagine what thought can be like all these things.
MARIA.   My thought was the moon. Julia, why is the moon like rain ?
JULIA.   Because it raises the rivers. You know the moon, acting on the waters, causes the tide to rise, and that the waters will rise also when swelled by the rain. Do not you recollect reading the other day in the newspaper an account of a great freshet, that overflowed the banks of a creek, and carried trees and houses away with it ?
MARIA.   Oh! yes; your explanation is very satisfactory.   And now, Louisa, why is the moon like a flower ?
LOUISA.   Because there is every day some change in it.
MARIA.   Charlotte, why is the moon like a bell ?

CHARLOTTE. A bell—a bell—I am sure I can never find any resemblance between the moon and a bell. I know not what to say. I give it up.

MARIA. Then you must pay a forfeit.

CHARLOTTE. Here, take my handkerchief.

MARIA. Sophia, why is the moon like an owl?

SOPHIA. Oh! that is easy enough. Because it does not appear in day-light.

MARIA. Helen, why is the moon like a star?

HELEN. Because it shines only at night. That comparison is very easy also.

MARIA. And now, Emily, why is the moon like a cheese?

CHARLOTTE. I suppose she will say, because it is in the shape of one.

EMILY. No, I will not; for a cheese is circular, but not globular. It is flat on both sides, and the moon is round like a ball.

CHARLOTTE. Well, I have seen little Dutch cheeses that are as round as balls.

EMILY. Pho—I will try to say something better than that. *(She pauses.)*

MARIA. Come, Emily, have you done considering?

EMILY. The moon is like a cheese, because it is largest in the east. That is, the moon looks largest when rising in the eastern part of the sky, and the largest cheeses are made in the eastern part of the Union.

MARIA. That's a very far-fetched explanation. However, we'll accept it. Julia, it is now your turn to have a thought.

JULIA. *(after a moment of meditation.)* Well then, Maria, what is my thought like?

MARIA. Like an amiable woman.

JULIA. You are next, Louisa.

LOUISA. Liké a large plum-cake.

JULIA. What is my thought like, Charlotte?

CHARLOTTE. Like sand.

JULIA. What is it like, Sophia ?

SOPHIA. Like a rose.

JULIA. Well, Helen ?

HELEN. Like dancing.

JULIA. And now, Emily, what is my thought like ?

EMILY. Like a lion.

JULIA. My thought is a rose.

SOPHIA. Ah ! a rose. How strange ?

JULIA. I have now to learn why a rose is like an amiable woman, a large plum-cake, sand, dancing, and a lion. Maria, what do you say ?

MARIA. The rose is like an amiable woman, because her sweetness remains long after her beauty has gone.

JULIA. Louisa, why is a rose like a large plum-cake.

LOUISA. Ah ! I am very much puzzled. Because roses and plum-cakes are indispensable at evening parties. I can think of nothing better.

JULIA. Well, Charlotte, why is a rose like sand ?

CHARLOTTE. Because it is easily scattered by the wind.

JULIA. Sophia, your comparison happened accidentally to be the same as my thought—a thing that very rarely occurs. However, when it does, the penalty is a forfeit.

SOPHIA. Do not call it the *penalty* ; for my having chanced unwittingly to fix upon a rose, as you did, is a misfortune, and not a fault. However, take my fan as a forfeit.

JULIA. Helen, why is a rose like dancing ?

HELEN. Because it is only becoming to young people.

JULIA. And why, Emily, is a rose like a lion ?

EMILY. Because it is one of the emblems of England.

41.

THE LAWYER.

This must be played by an odd number, as seven, nine, eleven, thirteen, that there may be one to personate the lawyer, after all the others have arranged themselves in pairs.

The company must seat themselves in two rows, facing each other, each girl taking for a partner the one opposite. She, that performs the lawyer, walks slowly between the lines, addressing a question to whichever she pleases. This question must not be answered by the one to whom it is addressed, but the reply must be made by her partner. If she inadvertently answers for herself, she must pay a forfeit; so also must her partner if she forgets or neglects to answer for her companion.

Example.

MARIA. Now let us arrange the chairs in two rows, that you may all take your seats facing each other. Julia, you shall be Harriet's partner; Louisa shall be Charlotte's; Helen shall be Emily's; and Matilda be Eliza's:—I will be the lawyer and ask the questions. Each must remember that she is not to reply herself, but she is to let her partner answer for her.

(They seat themselves in two rows. Maria goes to the head of the line, and stands first between Julia and Harriet.)

MARIA.   Julia, do you go into the country to-morrow ?

HARRIET.   No ; she does not go till Thursday.

MARIA.   Louisa, is your new work-box of velvet or morocco ?

CHARLOTTE.   Her new box is of beautiful painted velvet.

MARIA.   Helen, have you begun to learn French ?

EMILY.   Yes, she began last week.

MARIA.   Matilda, has your cut finger got well ?

ELIZA.   Not quite.

MARIA.   Eliza, what is your last new book ?

ELIZA.   Tales for Ellen.

MARIA.   Ah ! a forfeit.   You should have waited till Matilda re-
plied for you.

ELIZA.   There, there, you may take my shoe.

MARIA.   Eliza, which of the Tales for Ellen do you like best ?

MATILDA.   The Little Blue Bag.

ELIZA.   This time I was on my guard not to answer.

MARIA.   Emily, is not your frock too tight ?

HELEN.   No, quite the contrary.

MARIA.   Louisa, which do you prefer—maccaroons or rock-cakes ?

LOUISA.   Maccaroons, certainly.

MARIA.   A forfeit—a forfeit—you should not answer for yourself.

LOUISA.   Here is my waist-ribbon.   *(Taking it off.)*

MARIA.   Harriet, did you ever before play at the Lawyer ?

JULIA.   Yes, frequently.

5

42.

THE ELEMENTS.

A handkerchief is pinned up into the shape of a round ball. The girls sit in a circle. She, that is to begin the play, takes the ball and throws it to one of

her companions, calling out either " earth," " air," or
" water ;" fire being omitted, as that element has no
inhabitants. The girl to whom the ball is directed
must, on catching it, reply by giving the name of an
animal, proper to the element that has just been mentioned. If the word is " air," the answer must be
" eagle," " vulture," " hawk," or any other bird. If
the word is " water," the reply may be " whale,"
" shark," " porpoise." If the element is " earth,"
the answer must be the name of a beast, as " lion,"
" tiger," " bear," &c. If she that is addressed does
not reply promptly, or makes a mistake and names a
bird when she should have mentioned a beast, she is
to pay a forfeit. The one, that receives the ball, then
throws it to another, calling out one of the elements
and so the play goes round.

Examples.

MARIA. *(Throwing the ball to Helen.)* Earth!
HELEN. Panther. *(She throws the ball to Louisa.)* Air!
LOUISA. Woodpecker. *(She throws it to Julia.)* Water!
JULIA. Shad. *(Throws it to Sophia.)* Water!
SOPHIA. *(Starting.)* Oh! what am I thinking of! Turkey—
turkey—

MARIA. Ha, ha, ha! Do turkies live in the water?

SOPHIA. Oh! no. I meant turtle. However, I see I am too late. Here is this pencil as a forfeit. *(She throws the ball to Maria.)* Earth!

MARIA. Buffalo. *(Throwing the ball to Harriet.)* Air!

HARRIET. Mocking-bird. *(Throws the ball to Emily.)* Water!

EMILY. Rock-fish. *(Throwing the ball to Charlotte.)* Air!

CHARLOTTE. Duck.

HELEN. Now, Charlotte, that does not seem exactly right. A duck is a bird, to be sure, but does it ever fly in the air? Earth is its proper abode.

CHARLOTTE. You are very particular. Do not wild-ducks fly in the air? And very high too, and in large flocks.

HELEN. Then you should have said " wild-duck."

EMILY. And ducks also swim in the water.

MARIA. Well, I believe we must admit the word " duck" as a sufficiently good answer, whether the word is air, earth, or water; ducks being found in all those three elements.

HELEN. But always say " *wild*-duck," if the word is " air."

43.

THE SECRET WORD.

One of the company leaves the room, and the others fix on a word; such as " like," " care," " sight," " leave," " hear," &c. which is to be introduced into all their answers to the questions she must put to them on her return. When the word is decided on, she is called in, and asks a question of each in turn. In replying, every one must contrive to use the secret word without emphasizing or making it conspicuous. If the questioner remarks the frequent recurrence of the same word in the answers, she will easily be able to guess what it is. The one, from whose reply she has made the final discovery, then in her turn leaves the room while the next word is fixed on, and, on her return, becomes the questioner.

Example.

MARIA. Do you go out, Emily. *(Emily leaves the room.)* Now what shall be the word ?

HELEN. " Fear," or " love."

JULIA. Will not those words be too conspicuous ?   Let us try " like."

ALL. " Like—like"—let it be " like."   Come in, Emily

EMILY. *(returning.)*   Maria, do not you think the weather is very warm this evening ?

MARIA. Not warmer than I like it.

EMILY. Julia, are you fond of water-melon ?

JULIA. No—I like cantelope better.

EMILY. Helen, have you read Mrs. Hofland's Daughter of a Genius ?

HELEN. Yes, and I do not like it so well as her Son of a Genius.

EMILY. Matilda, were you up early this morning ?

MATILDA. Very early—I always like to rise with the lark.

EMILY. Harriet, did you make that reticule yourself ?

HARRIET. I did.   I like to make reticules, pincushions, needle-books, emery-bags, and every thing of the sort.

EMILY. " Like"—I have guessed it. " Like" is the word.

HARRIET. So it is.   Now I will go out.   *(She goes.)*

CHARLOTTE. " Saw"—let " saw" be the word.

MARIA. Very well.   Come in, Harriet.   *(Harriet comes in.)*

HARRIET. Maria, when did you see Clara Simmons ?

MARIA. I saw her the day before yesterday, when I was walking with Julia.

HARRIET. Julia, was Clara Simmons quite well ?

JULIA. Quite ; I never saw her look better.

HARRIET. Louisa, are you not very much pleased with your handsome new drawing-box?

LOUISA. Very much.   But I saw one in a store yesterday that was still more complete than mine.

HARRIET. Charlotte, are you acquainted with Laura Morton ?

CHARLOTTE. I saw her once at a dancing-school ball, but I have no acquaintance with her.

HARRIET. Emily, do not you think the new table in your honey-suckle arbour is quite too high ?

EMILY. Yes ; but the carpenter is coming to-morrow to saw off a piece from each leg, and then it will be a proper height.

HARRIET. " Saw"—" saw" is the word.

MARIA. Ha, ha, ha ! Emily, you had better not have used the word *saw* in that sense. You see, Harriet guessed it immediately.

EMILY. No matter. I have not the least objection to going out again.

44.

MANY WORDS IN ONE.

One of the company having left the room, the others fix on a word for her to guess. The word may be " Cake." She is called in, and stops before the first one in the row, who says " Cap." She goes to the next, who says " Apple ;" the third says " Kettle," and the fourth says " Egg ;" each taking care to mention a word whose first letter is one that is found in the word " Cake," and to say them in regular order. The guesser, having heard all these words, pauses to think over their initial letters, and finds that, when put together, they are C,A,K,E, and compose

the word " Cake," which she immediately pronounces ·
and it is then the turn of the one at the head of the
row to go out while a word is proposed.   If most of
the company are unacquainted with the play, the one
at the head need not explain at first the manner in
which the word is guessed ; but she had better tell
her companions beforehand what words they are to
say when the guesser comes in, and then they will all
be surprised at her guessing, not thinking that it is
from putting together the initial letters.

𝔈𝔵𝔞𝔪𝔭𝔩𝔢.

MARIA.   Julia, you know this play, so you had better be the first to
go out. (Julia leaves the room.)   Now we will fix on the word
Rainbow for Julia to guess.   Are any of you acquainted with the
play ?
ALL.   I am not—I am not—
MARIA.   Very well, then I will tell you what words to say when Julia presents herself before you. If you all knew the play you might
choose your own words.   I myself will say " Rose." Sophia do you say
" Arrow."   Emily your word may be " Ice."   Caroline's may be
" Nutmeg."   Louisa's   may be " Bonnet."   Charlotte's may be
" Orange," and Harriet may say " Wafer."   Come in, Julia. Now be
sure to remember your words.   (Julia returns.) Well, Julia, my word
is Rose.
    (Julia goes all along the row, and as she stops before each,
        they say the word allotted to them.)
SOPHIA.   Arrow.

EMILY. Ice.

CAROLINE. Nutmeg.

LOUISA. Bonnet.

CHARLOTTE. Orange.

HARRIET. Wafer.

(Julia pauses a moment, and finds that the initial letters of all these words make R A I N B O W.)

JULIA. Rainbow—the word is Rainbow.

ALL. So it is—

CAROLINE. I cannot imagine how you could find it out.

EMILY. I think I can guess the mode of discovery. However I will not disclose it.

HARRIET. I believe I can guess it too. But I also will not tell.

CHARLOTTE. Well it is a mystery to me.

JULIA. It will not be when the play has gone on a little longer. You will find it out by practice. Come, Maria, you are to be the next guesser.

45.

THE WATCH-WORD.

One of the company must leave the room, while another touches some article in her absence, which she must endeavour to guess on her return. Before her departure, the mistress of the play takes her aside and whispers to her the watch-word, meaning that when she hears her ask, " is it *this* ?" she may be sure that she points to the object which has been actually touched ; but, on the other hand, the question " is it *that* ?" refers to things that have not been touched.

Example.

MARIA. Louisa, do you go out, but first let me say something to you in private. *(She takes Louisa aside, and whispers to her, saying,)* Julia will touch something while you are gone, and when, on your return, I point to different things and ask, " is it *that* ?" you may be sure I am not directing you to the right object, and you must say " no." But when I ask, " is it *this* ?" you may say, " yes," for you may be sure that I then mean the thing that Julia has actually touched. Go now, remember that the watch-word is " *this*," and reply accordingly. *(Louisa goes out.)* Come, Julia, what will you touch ?

JULIA. There, I touch the work-basket. Come in, Louisa. *(Louisa returns.)*

MARIA. *(Pointing to a book.)* Is it that ?

LOUISA. No.

MARIA. *(Showing a pin-cushion.)* Is it that ?

LOUISA. No.

MARIA. *(Pointing to a newspaper.)* Is it that ?

LOUISA. No.

MARIA. *(Showing a work-box.)* Is it that ?

LOUISA. No.

MARIA. *(Pointing to a basket.)* Is it *this* ?

LOUISA. Yes. *(The other girls, being unacquainted with the play, look surprised.)*

CHARLOTTE. Well, it really *was* the basket that Julia touched.

HELEN. How could Louisa possibly know ?

HARRIET. How could she be sure that Julia had not touched any of the other things that were mentioned ?

MARIA. Well, Harriet, you shall go out next. So first come aside with me, and I will let you into the secret. [By the bye it must be remembered, that, in this play, no one goes out twice.]

(She takes Harriet to the other end of the room, and whispers to her that the watch-word will now be " THAT." Harriet goes out, and, while she is away, Charlotte touches the lamp ; and on her return, Maria questions her for awhile by asking, " is it this ?" to which, of course, Harriet answers, " no ;" but when Maria inquires, " is it THAT ?" as she points to the lamp, Harriet knows that she may say " yes.")

46.

THE NEWSPAPER.

This play seems, at first, to be very trifling and ridiculous, but, if well managed, it is extremely diverting, and excites much laughter. Any number may engage in it.

One is appointed to read the newspaper, and each of the others chooses a trade ; for instance, that of baker, butcher, tailor, shoemaker, or grocer. They all seat themselves in a row, or in a half circle, and the reader takes her place in front. She selects from the paper a piece of news (the more important the better), and reads it in an audible and distinct voice, stopping frequently in the midst of a sentence and looking steadfastly at one of her companions. She that is looked at by the reader must instantly fill up the pause with one or two words, which refer to the trade she has chosen. The reader then proceeds to finish the sentence and begin another, stopping at intervals as before ; her companions, each as she looks at them, supplying the pauses with some allusion to their trades. Whoever is unable to do so, promptly and without mistake, must pay a forfeit.

Example.

MARIA. Come, dear girls, take your seats. Here is a newspaper, containing an account of the French Revolution of July,

1830. I am going to read—therefore make haste and choose your trades.

JULIA. I will keep a china-store.

SOPHIA. I'll be a grocer.

EMILY. I a cook.

LOUISA. I'll keep a dry-goods store.

CHARLOTTE. I will be a butcher.

CLARA. And I a mantua-maker.

MARIA. *(Reading the newspaper.*)* " Early in the morning, the whole"—*(looking at Julia)*—

JULIA. Dinner-set—

MARIA. "Was in motion. Detachments from the suburbs had put themselves in "

SOPHIA. Vinegar.

MARIA. " Armed citizens occupied the "—

EMILY. Frying-pans.

MARIA. " Others had taken possession of the "—

---

* " Early in the morning, the whole *population of Paris* was in motion. Detachments from the suburbs had put themselves in *march ;* armed citizens occupied the *Hotel de Ville.* Others had taken possession of the *passages of Notre Dame,* planted the *tri-coloured flag,* and sounded the *tocsin.* All were prepared to fight. All the powder and lead which they found in the shops was taken. The entire Polytechnic school came out to *fight.* The students of Law and Medicine imitated the *example.* In fact, Paris appeared like a camp. All the shops were *closed ;* and royal guards, lancers, Swiss, and *regiments of the line,* were drawn up on all sides."

LOUISA. Cotton balls.

MARIA. " Planted the"—

CHARLOTTE. Marrow-bones.

MARIA. " And sounded the "

CLARA. Scissars.

MARIA. " All were prepared to "—

JULIA. Break tumblers.

MARIA. " All the powder and lead, which they found in the"—

SOPHIA. Molasses—

MARIA. " Was taken. The entire Polytechnic School came out to "—

EMILY. Make gingerbread.

MARIA. " The students of Law and Medicine imitated the "

LOUISA. Worked-muslin.

MARIA. " In fact, Paris appeared like a "

CHARLOTTE. Chopping-block.

MARIA. " All the shops were "—

CLARA. Cut bias.

MARIA. " And royal-guards, lancers, Swiss and "

JULIA. Tea-pots—

MARIA. " Were drawn up on all sides."

47.

THE MERCHANTS.

Each of the company in turn calls herself a merchant, and mentions an article that she has for sale.

The one next to her must say whether that article is animal, vegetable, or mineral. If she makes a mistake, she loses her turn. If she answers rightly, she becomes the next merchant, and proposes something for sale, asking also if it is animal, vegetable, or mineral ; and in this manner the play goes round.

Example.

MARIA. I am a China merchant, and have a tea-set to sell. Is it animal, vegetable, or mineral ?

LOUISA. Mineral. China is made of clay and flint and things belonging to earth.——Now it is my turn. I am a dry-goods merchant, and have a piece of gingham to sell ; is it animal, vegetable, or mineral ?

HELEN. Vegetable ; gingham being made of cotton.——I keep a grocery store, and have a box of candles to sell ; are they animal, vegetable, or mineral ?

CHARLOTTE. Animal. Candles are made either of tallow, spermaceti, or wax, all of which are animal substances.——I keep a cabinet-warehouse, and have a dining-table for sale ; is it animal, vegetable, or mineral ?

HARRIET. Vegetable ; being made of the wood of the mahogany tree.——I am a silk-mercer, and have a piece of satin for sale ; is it animal, mineral, or vegetable ?

CAROLINE. Vegetable.

HARRIET. What—satin, vegetable? Is it not made of silk thread, produced by the silk-worm? therefore it must be animal. Caroline, you have lost your turn, and can sell nothing this time. Come, Emily, you are merchant now.

EMILY. I am a stationer, and have a quire of letter-paper for sale; is it animal, vegetable, or mineral?

JULIA. Vegetable; white paper being made of linen or cotton rags.——I am a druggist, and have some opium to sell; is it animal, mineral, or vegetable?

MATILDA. Mineral.

MARIA. Oh! no, no. Opium is vegetable; it is the congealed juice of the poppy. You have lost your turn of being merchant, Matilda, and it has now come to me again.

MATILDA. I thought almost all medicines were minerals.

MARIA. A large proportion of them are; but a very great number of drugs are the produce of plants, and therefore vegetable.

48.

TEA TABLE.

The children form a circle, the name of an article belonging to the tea-table having been given to each, as Tea, Toast, Butter, Sugar, Cream, &c. The one named Tea begins by whirling round on one foot and saying, " I turn Tea, who turns Sugar?" Sugar replies by turning Cream, or any one she pleases. If

6

the one that is turned does not answer promptly, or forgets her name, she pays a forfeit.

Example.

MARIA.   Now, Harriet, you shall be Tea ; Julia shall be Cream ; Helen, Sugar ; Louisa, Butter ; Charlotte, Bread ; Caroline, Cake ; Emily shall be Honey ; and I will be Sliced Ham.   Come, let all stand up in a ring.

(Harriet whirls round, saying, " I turn Tea, who turns Cream ?"

JULIA.   I turn Cream, who turns Sugar ?
HELEN.   I turn Sugar, who turns Bread ?
CHARLOTTE.   I turn Bread, who turns Butter ?
LOUISA.   I turn Butter, who turns Cake ?
CAROLINE.   I turn Cake, who turns Honey ?
EMILY.   I turn Honey, who turns Ham ?   No one answers.   Who turns Ham ?   Ah ! Maria, a forfeit.   You forget that you are Ham.
MARIA.   I was thinking of something else.   Well, I deserve the penalty, for we ought to pay proper attention to whatever we are doing, even when it is only play.   I give this book as a forfeit, and will take care to avoid incurring another.

49.

MY LADY'S TOILET.

This play is somewhat similar to the last.   To each of the company is given the name of an article of dress.   If eight girls are playing, all the chairs, except seven, must be taken out of the room, or set aside in one place in one place with their backs outward ; so as to leave one chair too few. All the girls then seat themselves round the room ; except one, who is called the Lady's Maid and stands in the centre. The maid calls out, " My lady's up, and wants her Shoes." She, of that name, starts up and exclaims " Shoes," seating herself again immediately. Then the maid says, " My lady's up, and wants her Gown." Gown directly answers to her name ; and so on till all the articles are called over and answered. If any one fails to rise and reply quickly, she pays a forfeit.

Occasionally, the maid exclaims, " My lady wants her whole Toilet ;" and then every one quits her chair, and runs to change her seat by taking another. As there is a chair too few, one of the girls is of course left without a seat in the scramble, and she becomes the Lady's Maid ; and takes her place in the middle of the room to call the names of the others.

Example.

MARIA. Now, as there are seven of us, we must have but six chairs ; so let us take all the others, and set them at the other end of the room, turning their fronts to the wall. *(They fix the chairs.)* Come, Julia, you shall be Scarf ; Matilda shall be Collar ; Charlotte, Frock ; Harriet, Belt ; Louisa, Cap ; Emily, Bonnet ; and I will be

Lady's Maid.   Now all take your seats.   *(They seat themselves.)*
My lady's up, and wants her collar.

MATILDA. *(rising.)* Collar !

MARIA. My lady's up, and wants her frock.

CHARLOTTE. Frock !

MARIA. My lady's up, and wants her scarf.

JULIA. Scarf !

MARIA. My lady's up, and wants her cap.

LOUISA. Cap !

MARIA. My lady's up, and wants her bonnet.   Bonnet—bonnet—
Why, Emily, you do not answer.   You have not your wits about you.

EMILY. What could I be thinking of ?   My handkerchief must be
my forfeit.

MARIA. My lady's up, and wants her scarf.

JULIA. Scarf !

MARIA. My lady's up, and wants her scarf.   Julia—Julia—have
you forgotten already that you are scarf ?

JULIA. Why I was the last that answered, and I did not think you
would call my name again immediately.

MARIA. Oh ! yes—It's not contrary to rule, and it makes the play
more diverting.   You know in Tea-table also, we may call the same
name twice successively.   Come, where is your forfeit ?

JULIA. This little nosegay.

MARIA. My lady's up, and wants her belt.

HARRIET. Belt !

MARIA. My lady's up, and wants her belt.

HARRIET. Belt !   You see, I have *my wits* about me.

MARIA. My lady wants her whole toilet.

> *(They all quit their seats, and run to other chairs.   Julia is left
> out as Lady's Maid.   As soon as they are all quietly seated,
> she calls for the whole toilet again, and there is a second scram-
> ble and changing of seats.   Emily is next left out, and becomes
> Lady's Maid.)*

50.

THE DUMB ORATOR.

In this amusement there are in reality two per-
formers, one that speaks without gesture, and one
that makes gestures without speaking. We will suppose that Maria personates the speaker. She stands
in the middle of the room, inveloped in a large cloak,

Harriet hides behind her, concealed under the same
cloak, keeping down her head below Maria's shoulders.   She must thrust out her arms through the
arm-holes of the cloak, while Maria's arms must remain motionless down at her sides.

When all is ready, Maria must recite with great
energy some popular speech, such as are found in
school-books on elocution ; for instance, Lady Ran-
dolph's Soliloquy, Young Norval's story of himself,
or something similar.   One that admits of considerable action is always to be preferred.   Maria, while
repeating the speech, must keep perfectly still ; and
Harriet, with her hands and arms protruding from
the cloak must "make all the motions."   These
motions should be as laughable and ridiculous as
possible ; so as to burlesque the speech.   She should
spread out her arms, wave her hands, point upwards
and downwards, strike Maria on the forehead and
breast, and exaggerate every gesture in the most ludicrous manner.

The Dumb Orator (when humorously performed)
is a more diverting exhibition that can possibly be
imagined by those who have never seen it

In case my young readers should not be acquainted with the popular speech of Young Norval (as referred to in the foregoing article) we will here insert it. It is from Mr Home's tragedy of Douglas.

My name is Norval ; on the Grampian hills
My father feeds his flocks ; a frugal swain,
Whose constant cares were to increase his store,
And keep his only son, myself, at home.
For I had heard of battles, and I long'd
To follow to the field some warlike lord ;
And Heaven soon granted what my sire denied.
This moon, which rose last night round as my shield,
Had not yet filled her horns, when by her light,
A band of fierce barbarians, from the hills,
Rush'd like a torrent down upon the vale,
Sweeping our flocks and herds.   The shepherds fled
For safety and for succour.   I alone,
With bended bow and quiver full of arrows,
Hover'd about the enemy, and mark'd
The road he took : then hasten'd to my friends ;
Whom, with a troop of fifty chosen men,
I met advancing.   The pursuit I led,
Till we o'ertook the spoil-encumber'd foe.
We fought and conquer'd.   Ere a sword was drawn,
An arrow from my bow had pierced their chief,
Who wore that day the arms which now I wear.
Returning home in triumph, I disdained
The shepherd's slothful life ; and having heard
That our good king had summon'd his bold peers
To lead their warriors to the Carron side,

I left my father's house, and took with me
A chosen servant to conduct my steps ;
Yon trembling coward, who forsook his master !
   Journeying with this intent, I pass'd these towers,
And, Heaven-directed, came this day to do
The happy deed that gilds my humble name.

This well-known speech is much in favour with
juvenile orators, as it relates a story and admits of
considerable gesture.

51.

CONSEQUENCES.

This is best played by three persons, though four
or two may engage in it.   First prepare some white
pasteboard or some blank cards by cutting them into
small slips, all of one size.   There should at least be
four dozen slips ; but eight dozen will be better still,
as the game will then be longer and more varied.
We will, however, suppose that there are four dozen
slips of card.   First take twenty-four of these slips
and write upon each, as handsomely and legibly as
you can, the name of one of your acquaintances.
Then take twelve more cards and write on each the
name of a place, as " in the street," " in church," " in

the garden," " in the orchard," " at a ball," "at school," &c. Lastly on the remaining dozen of cards write the consequences, or what happened to the young ladies. You may say for instance, "They lost their shoes," "They tore their gloves," "They took offence," or something similar. The consequences should be so contrived that none of them will appear absurd and unmeaning with reference to the places.

When the cards are all ready (and when once made they will last a long time), the play may begin by Julia taking the two dozen that have the names (two names being read together) ; Sophia taking the dozen that designates the places, and Harriet taking charge of the consequence. Each had better put her cards into a small basket, from which they are to be drawn out as they chance to come uppermost. Or they may be well shuffled and laid in a pile before each of the players, with the blank sides upwards. They must be shuffled every game.

Example.

Julia, Sophia, Harriet.

JULIA. Well, are we all ready ? Come, then, let us begin. *(She takes up two cards and reads them.)* " Louisa Hartley and Helen Wallis"—

SOPHIA. *(reading a card.)* Were together " in a sleigh."

HARRIET. *(reading.)* The consequence was, " they caught cold."

JULIA. " Emily Campbell and Clara Nelson"

SOPHIA. Were both " at a ball "

HARRIET. The consequence was " they were taken with fevers."

JULIA. " Maria Walden and Charlotte Rosewell"—

SOPHIA. Were together " in the street"—

HARRIET. The consequence was, " they got their feet wet."

JULIA. " Fanny Milford and Ellen Graves"—

SOPHIA. Were both " at a party"—

HARRIET. The consequence was, " their noses bled."

JULIA. " Amelia Temple and Caroline Douglas"—

SOPHIA. Were together " at the museum"—

HARRIET. The consequence was, " they were highly delighted."

JULIA. " Sophia Seymour and Harriet Harland"—

SOPHIA. Ah ! Harriet, your name and mine !—*(reading,)* were both in the kitchen."

HARRIET. The consequence was, " they did nothing at all."

JULIA. " Matilda Granby and Eliza Ross"—

SOPHIA. Were together " in the orchard."

HARRIET. The consequence was, " they quarrelled and parted."

JULIA. " Marianne Morley and Julia Gordon"—(that is myself)

SOPHIA. Were both " in church."

HARRIET. The consequence was, " they did not speak a word."

JULIA. " Adelaide Elmer and Juliet Fanning"—

SOPHIA. Were both " at the theatre."

HARRIET. The consequence was, " they were laughing all the time."

JULIA. " Georgiana Bruce and Eleanor Oakley"—

SOPHIA. Were " on the top of the house."

HARRIET. The consequence was, " they sprained their ankles."

JULIA. " Emmeline Stanley and Laura Lear"—

SOPHIA.   Were both " at school."

HARRIET.   The consequence was " they broke their bonnets."

JULIA.   " Margaret Ashwood and Lydia Bar clay"—

SOPHIA.   Were together " on a visit."

HARRIET.   " The consequence was, " they were glad to get home."

JULIA.   There now—we have gone through all the cards. So let us shuffle them, and begin another game. This time Sophia may take the names, Harriet the places, and I the consequences. I hope the answers this time also will be somewhat approp riate.

If you cannot conveniently procure white paste-board or blank cards, slips of thick white paper will do nearly as well. When not in use, they should be kept in a box.

Remember that, as two names are always read together, the number of names should be double that of the places and consequences.

Four persons may play this game by dividing the names between two, each of which will read one name. If played by two persons only, one must take all the names, the other must read both the places and consequences.

52.

I LOVE MY LOVE.

This may be played by any number, each taking a letter as it comes to her turn. Any mistake or hesitation incurs the penalty of a forfeit. She that begins may say,

A. I love my love with an A. because he is Artless—I hate him with an A. because he is Avaricious. He took me to the sign of the Anchor, and treated me to Apees and Almonds. His name is Abraham, and he comes from Albany.

B. I love my love with a B. because he is Brave. I hate him with a B. because he is Boisterous. He took me to the sign of the Bell, and treated me to Biscuits and Buns. His name is Benjamin and he comes from Boston.

C. I love my love with a C. because he is Candid. I hate him with a C. because he is Capricious. He took me to the sign of the Crow, and treated me to Cherries and Custards. His name is Charles, and he comes from Cincinnati.

D. I love my love with a D. because he is Diligent. I hate him with a D. because he is Disdainful. He took me to the sign of the Drum, and treated me to Damsons and Dough-nuts. His name is David, and he comes from Delaware.

E. I love my love with an E. because he is Elegant. I hate him with an E. because he is Envious. He took me to the sign of the Eagle, and treated me to Eels and Eggs. His name is Edward, and he comes from Easton.

F. I love my love with an F. because he is Faithful. I hate him with an F. because he is Foolish. He took me to the sign of the Fox, and treated me to Filberts and Figs. His name is Francis, and he comes from Farmington.

G. I love my love with a G. because he is Generous. I hate him with a G. because he is Graceless. He took me to the sign of the Grecian, and treated me to Grapes and Gooseberries. His name is Gustavus, and he comes from Georgia.

H. I love my love with an H. because he is Handsome. I hate him with an H. because he is Haughty. He took me to the sign of the Hunter and treated me to Ham and Hash. His name is Henry, and he comes from Harrisburgh.

I. I love my love with an I. because he is Ingenious. I hate him with an I. because he is Impertinent. He took me to the sign of the Indian, and treated me to Ice-cream and Isinglass Jelly. His name is Isaac, and he comes from Illinois.

J. I love my love with a J. because he is Judicious. I bate him with a J. because he is Jealous. He took me to the sign of the Judge, and treated me to Jelly and Jam. His name is James, and he comes from Jersey.

K. I love my love with a K. because he is kind. I hate him with a K. because he is Knavish. He took me to the sign of the King, and treated me to Kale and Kid. His name is Kenneth, and he comes from Kentucky.

L. I love my love with an L. because he is Liberal. I hate him with an L. because he is Listless. He took me to the sign of the Lion, and treated me to Lobster and Lamb. His name is Lewis, and he came from Lansingburgh.

M. I love my love with an M. because he is Modest. I hate him with an M. because he is Mischievous. He took me to the sign of the Mermaid, and treated me to Maccaroons and Marmelade. His name is Martin, and he comes from Marietta.

N. I love my love with an N. because he is Neat. I hate him with an N. because he is Noisy. He took me to the sign of the Nun, and treated me to Nuts and Nectarines. His name is Nathan, and he comes from Nashville.

O. I love my love with an O. because he is Obliging. I hate him with an O. because he is Officious. He took me to the sign of the Owl, and treated me to Oysters and Omelet. His name is Oliver, and he comes from Ohio.

P. I love my love with a P. because he is prudent. I hate him with a P. because he is Petulant. He took me to the sign of the Peacock, and treated me to Peaches and Plums. His name is Philip, and he comes from Pensacola.

Q. I love my love with a Q. because he is Quiet. I hate him with a Q. because he is Queer. He took me to the sign of the Quiver, and treated me with Quinces and Queen-cake. His name is Quintin, and he comes from Quebec.

R. I love my love with an R. because he is Regular. I hate him with an R. because he is Revengeful. He took me to the sign of the Rose, and treated me to Raisins and Rusk. His name is Richard, and he comes from Roanoke.

S. I love my love with an S. because he is Sensible. I hate him with an S. because he is Scornful. He took me to the sign of the Swan, and treated me to Strawberries and Syllabub. His name is Simon, and he comes from Sandusky.

T. I love my love with a T. because he is Temperate. I hate him with a T. because he is Treacherous. He took me to the sign of the Turk, and treated me to Terrapins and Turtle. His name is Timothy, and he comes from Tennessee.

U. is omitted.

V. I love my love with a V. because he is Valiant. I hate him with a V. because he is Vain. He took me to the sign of the Vine, and treated me to Venison and Veal. His name is Valentine, and he comes from Vermont.

W. I love my love with a W. because he is Witty. I hate him with a W. because he is Wild. He took me to the sign of the Waggon, and treated me to Water-melon and Walnuts. His name is William, and he comes from Washington.

X. Y. and Z. are always omitted, as it is impossible to find proper words beginning with those letters.

————

For the above words, others beginning with the same letters may be substituted at the pleasure of the players. For instance, in the letter A. the words may be, " Active—Artful—sign of the Antelope—Anchovies and Ale—Adam—Annapolis" :—or for the letter B. " Bountiful—Barbarous—sign of the Bear—Beacon and Beans—Benedict—Burlington."

It may be more diverting for the treat to consist of things totally opposite and unsuitable—as—" Cabbage and Cheese"—" Molasses and Mutton"—" Sausages and Sugar"—" Oranges and Oil"—&c.

53.

ANOTHER WAY OF PLAYING MY LOVE.

A. I love my love with an A. because he is Amusing. I will send him to Alabama, and feed him with Apples ; I will give him an Axe to cut down his trees with, and a bunch of Acorns for a nosegay.

B. I love my love with a B. because he is Beautiful. I will send him to Buffalo, and feed him with Buckwheat cakes ; I will give him a Bag for his money, and a bunch of Broom-corn for a nosegay.

C. I love my love with a C. because he is Careful. I will send him to Connecticut, and feed him on Cod-fish. I will give him a Cloak to wear in cold weather, and a bunch of Celery for a nosegay.

D. I love my love with a D. because he is Diffident. I will send him to Dartmouth, and feed him with Dumplings. I will give him a Diamond to cut glass with, and a bunch of Dock-leaves for a nosegay.

E. I love my love with an E. because he is Entertaining. I will send him to Emmetsburgh, and feed him with Egg-sauce. I will give him an Earthen-pitcher to fetch water in, and a bunch of Elder-berries for a nosegay.

F. I love my love with an F. because he is Friendly. I will send him to Falmouth, and feed him with Fritters. I will give him a Fife to play on, and a bunch of Flax for a nosegay.

G. I love my love with a G. because he is Good-natured. I will send him to Georgetown, and feed him with Gingerbread. I will give him a Gun to shoot squirrels with, and a bunch of Grass for a nosegay.

H. I love my love with an H. because he is Humble. I will send him to Hackensack, and feed him on Herrings. I will give him a Hat because his old one is worn out, and a bunch of Hops for a nosegay.

I. I love my love with an I. because he is Industrious. I will send him to Indiana, and feed him on Indian-pudding. I will give him an Ink-stand to write letters with, and a bunch of Ivy for a nosegay.

J. I love my love with a J. because he is Just. I will send him to Juniata and feed him on Johnny-cake. I will give him a Jew's-harp to play on, and a bunch of Juniper for a nosegay.

K. I love my love with a K. because he is Knowing. I will send him to Kinderhook, and feed him with Ketchup. I will give him a Knapsack to put his clothes in, and a bunch of Kale for a nosegay.

L. I love my love with an L. because he is Lively. I will send him to Lousiana, and feed him on Lemons. I will give him Leather for his shoes, and a bunch of Lettuce for a nosegay.

M. I love my love with an M. because he is Merciful. I will send him to Marblehead, and feed him on Mushrooms. I will give him a Mill to grind his coffee in, and a bunch of Marjoram for a nosegay.

N. I love my love with an N. because he is Nice. I will send him to Nantucket and feed him on Nutmegs. I will give him a set of Nine-pins to play with, and a bunch of Nettles for a nosegay.

O. I love my love with an O. because he is Obedient. I will send him to Oswego, and feed him on Onions. I will give him some Oil for his lamp, and a bunch of Oats for a nosegay.

P. I love my love with a P. because he is Peaceable. I will send him to Poughkeepsie, and feed him on Pickles. I will give him a Patch to mend his coat with, and a bunch of Pokeberries for a nosegay.

D. I love my love with a Q. because he is Quick. I will send him to Queenstown and feed him on Quails. I will give him a Quilt for his bed, and a bunch of Quills for a nosegay.

7

R.   I love my love with an R. because he is Reasonable.   I will send him to Roxbury, and feed him on Rabbits.   I will give him a Rail to mend his fence, and a bunch of Rye for a nosegay.

S.   I love my love with an S. because he is Steady.   I will send him to Salem, and feed him on Salad.   I will give him some Soap to wash his hands with, and a bunch of Sumach for a nosegay.

T.   I love my love with a T. because he is Thoughtful.   I will send him to Trenton, and feed him on Turnips.   I will give him a Trap to catch his mice in, and a bunch of Thistles for a nosegay.

U.   Is omitted.

V.   I love my love with a V. because he is Virtuous.   I will send him to Virginia and feed him on Vermicelli.   I will give him a Violin to play on, and a bunch of Vine-leaves for a nosegay.

W.   I love my love with a W. because he is Wise.   I will send him to Wilmington, and feed him on Waffles.   I will give him a Waistcoat to wear at his wedding, and a bunch of Wormwood for a nosegay.

X. Y. and Z. are omitted.

This, like the one similar, may be played by any number.   Mis-spelling, or any other mistake, is punished by a forfeit.   For the foregoing words any others may be substituted according to the taste of the player, provided that they are appropriate.   The more ridiculous, the more amusing.

These alphabetical plays, though many grown persons may consider them foolish, are in fact not only diverting but very improving to children.

54.

CUPID.

The mistress of the play seats herself at one end of the room. At the other end her companions range themselves in a row, each coming forward in turn and addressing her in the character of Cupid, and afterwards taking a station behind her. Every one, as she personates Cupid, must adapt her countenance and gestures to the manner in which she describes him. She who fails to do so, but merely repeats her words without the proper expression or attitude, is to pay a forfeit. Each takes a letter till the whole alphabet is completed ; the first girl, for instance, saying, Cupid comes Affable.

A. Cupid comes Affable—or Affected—or Angry.
B. Cupid comes Begging—Bouncing—Backwards.
C. Cupid comes Capering—Crying—Chilly—Creeping.
D. Cupid comes Dancing—Dull—Downcast.
E. Cupid comes Eating—Eagerly—Exasperated.

F.   Cupid comes Frightened—Fatigued—Fighting.
G.   Cupid comes Gaily—Gravely—Grieving—Gliding.
H.   Cupid comes Haughty—Hastily—Heedless—Hobbling.
I.   Cupid comes Indolent—Impudent.
J.   Cupid comes Jumping—Jealous—Joyful.
K.   Cupid comes Kissing.
L.   Cupid comes Laughing—Limping—Loitering.
M.   Cupid comes Mournful—Majestic—Meekly.
N.   Cupid comes Noisy—Negligent.
O.   Cupid comes Outrageous—Orderly.
P.   Cupid comes Peaceful—Peevish—Playful—Painful.
Q.   Cupid comes Quickly—Quarrelsome—Quizzical.
R.   Cupid comes Raging—Respectfully—Rustic.
S.   Cupid comes Smiling—Sighing—Skipping—Sideways.
T.   Cupid comes Trembling—Tiptoe—Thoughtful—Twining.
U.   Cupid comes Upright—Unhappy—Unruly.
V.   Cupid comes Violently—Volatile.
W.   Cupid comes Whimpering—Weary—Woful.
X.   Is omitted.
Y.   Cupid comes Yawning.
Z.   Cupid comes Zigzag.

A little reflection will soon show in what manner Cupid is to be performed under all these various aspects, and in this way the alphabet may be gone over three or four times, always changing the words when practicable. Smart children find this play very amusing.

55.

SELLING FORFEITS OR PAWNS.

When a sufficient number of forfeits or pawns
have been collected during the play, it is time to sell
them. For this purpose, one of the girls is seated on
a chair in the middle of the room and blindfolded.

Another stands behind her with the basket, containing the pawns ; and taking out one at a time, she holds it up, asking, "What is to be done to the owner of this ?" She that is blindfolded inquires, "Is it fine or superfine ?" meaning "Does it belong to a young gentleman or to a young lady ?" If the owner is a female, the reply must be, "It is superfine." Then the seller of the forfeits (still remaining blindfolded) must decide what the owner must do before the pawn can be restored to her.

Examples.

FIRST.

The first may be what is called performing a statue.

The owner of the forfeit is to stand on a chair in the middle of the room ; and every one, in turn, is to put her in a different position. One is to make her raise her hands above her head and clasp them together ; another is to place her arms behind her, grasping her elbows with her hands ; a third makes the statue clasp her hands on her breast ; a fourth re-

PERFORMING A STATUE.

quires her to hold out her dress, as if she was just going to dance ; a fifth desires her to cover her eyes with her hands ; and so on, till each has placed the statue in a different attitude. After which, she descends from her pedestal and the forfeit is restored to her.

SECOND.

The owner of the pawn is to be fed with water till she guesses who is feeding her. For this purpose she is blindfolded, and seated on a chair. A glass of water with a tea-spoon in it is prepared, and each girl, in turn, puts a spoonful of water into the mouth of her blindfolded companion, who must endeavour to guess who is doing it. Whenever she guesses rightly, the bandage is removed, and the forfeit is restored to her.

THIRD.

She shall be carried three times round the room on a seat, formed of the arms of two of her companions, who are to say as they carry her, " Give me a pin to stick in the cushion that carries my lady to London." They cross their arms, holding each other by the wrists, and she that is carried throws an arm round the neck of each.

FOURTH.

She must recite a verse of poetry, which had better be something diverting or humorous.

FIFTH.

She must keep a serious face for five minutes,

without either smiling or frowning, let the company do as they will.

SIXTH.

She must repeat five times rapidly, without mispronouncing a letter, " Villy Vite and his Vife vent a voyage to Vinsor and Vest Vickham von Vitsun Vednesday."

SEVENTH.

Laugh in one corner of the room, cry in another, yawn in the third corner, and dance in the fourth.

EIGHTH.

Bite an inch off the poker. This is done by making a bite at the distance of an inch from the poker. If there is no poker at hand, an umbrella or a stick will do as well.

NINTH.

Repeat as follows, three times successively, without a pause or a blunder ·

" Peter Piper pick'd a peck of pickle-peppers,
A peck of pickle-peppers Peter Piper pick'd ;
If Peter Piper pick'd a peck of pickle-peppers,
Where's the peck of pickle-peppers Peter Piper pick'd ?"

TENTH.

Say this correctly, without stopping :

" Bandy-legg'd Borachio Mustachio Whiskerifusticus the Bald and brave Bombardino of Bagdad helped Abomilique Blue-Beard Bashaw of Babelmandel to beat down an abominable Bumble Bee at Balsora."

ELEVENTH.

Kiss a box, inside and outside, without opening it. That is, first kiss the box inside of the room, and then take it outside of the room and kiss it there also.

TWELFTH.

Answer five questions while another chucks you under the chin.

THIRTEENTH.

Ask a question of one of the company, which they can only answer by saying " Yes." The question is, " What does Y, E, S, spell ?"

FOURTEENTH.

Kneel to the wittiest in the room, bow or curtsy to the prettiest, and kiss the one you love best.

FIFTEENTH.

Make a good cat's cradle.

SIXTEENTH.

Tell a riddle or conundrum.

SEVENTEENTH.

Hop, on one foot, four times round the room.

EIGHTEENTH.

Kiss some one through the tongs.

NINETEENTH.

Count twenty backwards.

TWENTIETH.

Show four bare legs.   That is, turn a chair upside down, so as to display its four legs.

TWENTY-FIRST.

Tell a short story, or anecdote.

TWENTY-SECOND.

Sing a short song.

TWENTY-THIRD.

Dance a solo or hornpipe.

TWENTY-FOURTH.

Put yourself through the key-hole.   This is done by writing the word " yourself " on a small slip of paper, rolling it up, and putting it through the key-hole.

Repeat these three lines rapidly, without a pause or a mistake :

> " As I went in the garden, I saw five brave maids
> Sitting on five broad beds, braiding broad braids. '
> I said to these five brave maids, sitting on five broad beds
> Braiding broad braids, " Braid broad braids, brave maids."

Kiss yourself in the looking-glass.

Guess a riddle or conundrum.

Spell " *new door*" in one word. This is done by writing on a slate or piece of paper " *one word*." It will be seen that " new door" and " one word" con-tain exactly the same letters, though differently ar-ranged.

Repeat the " twine-twister," as follows ·

" When the twister a twisting will twist him a twine,
For the twisting his twist he three times doth entwist ;
But, if one of the twines of the twist doth untwine,
The twine that untwisteth untwisteth the twine.
Untwisting the twine that untwisteth between,
He twirls with his twister the two in a twine ;
Then twice having twisted the twines of the twine,
He twisteth the twine he hath twined in twain :
The twain, that in twining before in the twine
As twines were intwisted, he now doth untwine.
'Twixt the twain intertwisting a twine more between,
He, twirling his twister, makes a twist of the twine."

THIRTY.

Immediately after "the twine-twister" has been said, the next pawn may be redeemed by desiring the owner to spell all this in seven letters ; which is done by spelling A,L,L, T,H,I,S.

THIRTY-FIRST.

Write your name in one letter. This is done by writing on a slate, or on paper with a lead-pencil, one very large letter, introducing in it your own name, written small, thus ·

THIRTY-SECOND.

Decypher two lines, addressed by a boy to his school-master. The following lines must be written by some one who knows how, and the owner of the pawn must write under them the explanation

$$2 \ + \ u \quad r \quad 2 \ + \ u \quad b$$
$$I \quad c \quad u \quad r \quad 2 \ + \ for \quad me.$$

The explanation is :

Too cross you are, too cross you be,
I see you are too cross for me.

THIRTY-THIRD.

Decypher the schoolmaster's answer to the boy :

$$2 \quad yy \quad u \quad r \quad 2 \quad yy \quad u \quad b$$
$$I \quad c \quad u \quad r \quad 2 \quad yy \quad for \quad me.$$

This is the explanation :

Too wise you are, too wise you be,
I see you are too wise for me.

THIRTY-FOURTH.

Perform a Dutch doll.

THIRTY-FIFTH.

Perform the Dumb Orator.

Repeat the list of

WONDERFUL SIGHTS.

I saw a peacock with a fiery tail,
I saw a blazing comet pour down hail,
I saw a cloud all wrapp'd with ivy round,
I saw a lofty oak creep on the ground,
I saw a beetle swallow up a whale,
I saw the foaming sea brimful of ale,
I saw a china mug fifteen feet deep,
I saw a well full of men's tears that weep,
I saw wet eyes all of a flaming fire,
I saw a house high as the moon and higher,
I saw the sun e'en at the dead midnight,
I saw the man that saw these awful sights.

Or this

MORE WONDERS.

I saw a pack of cards gnawing a bone,
I saw a dog seated on Britain's throne,
I saw king George shut up within a box,
I saw a shilling driving a fat ox,
I saw a man laying in a muff all night,
I saw a glove reading news by candle-light,
I saw a woman not a twelvemonth old,
I saw a great coat all of solid gold,
I saw two buttons telling of their dreams,
I heard my friends, who wish'd I'd quit these themes.

Repeat the Wonderful Sights so as to make them no wonders at all. This is done by altering the punctuation—thus :

> I saw a peacock ;—with a fiery tail
> I saw a comet ;—pour down hail
> I saw a cloud ;—wrapp'd with ivy round
> I saw a lofty oak ;—creep on the ground
> I saw a beetle ;—swallow up a whale
> I saw the foaming sea ;—brimful of ale
> I saw a china mug ;—fifteen feet deep
> I saw a well ;—full of men's tears that weep
> I saw wet eyes ;—high as the moon and higher
> I saw the sun ;—even at the dark midnight
> I saw the man that saw these awful sights.

MORE WONDERS, EXPLAINED.

> I saw a pack of cards ;—gnawing a bone
> I saw a dog ;—seated on Britain's throne
> I saw king George ;—shut up within a box
> I saw a shilling ;—driving a fat ox
> I saw a man ;—laying in a muff all night
> I saw a glove ;—reading news by candle-light
> I saw a woman ;—not a twelvemonth old
> I saw a great coat ;—all of solid gold
> I saw two buttons ;—telling of their dreams
> I heard my friends, who wish'd I'd quit these themes.

Get a sixpence off your forehead, without putting

your hands to it. This is done as follows :—The mistress of the play takes a sixpence or fivepenny bit, and wetting it with her tongue, pretends to stick it very fast on the forehead of the owner of the pawn. In reality she withdraws it immediately, and conceals it in her own hand ; but makes the owner of the pawn believe that it is all the time on her forehead ; and she is easily deceived, as she is not permitted to put up her hand to feel ; and all the company humour the joke, and pretend that the sixpence is actually sticking there. She shakes her head, and tries every means (except the interdicted) to make the sixpence drop off, wondering she does not see it fall, and amazed that it sticks so fast, supposing it to be really on her forehead. No one must undeceive her. Whenever she discovers the trick, and finds that in reality there is nothing on her forehead, her forfeit may be restored to her. If she puts up her hand to feel for the sixpence, she must pay another pawn.

THIRTY-NINTH.

Stand in the corner till some one prevails on you to come out, though all your answers must be " No." The dialogue, that ought to take place, is as follows,

8

or something to this effect ; but it may be varied, according to the ingenuity of the questioner :—

" Do you wish to remain in the corner ?"

" No."

" Is it very irksome to you ?"

" No."

" Shall I lead you out in half an hour ?"

" No."

" Are you willing to stay here all night ?"

" No."

" Shall I go away, and leave you here ?"

" No."

" Will you remain in the corner another moment ?"

" No."

The answer to the last question implies a consent to quit the corner immediately, therefore you must be led out.

FORTIETH.

Walk three times round the room with a boy's hat on your head, and bow to the company as you take it off.

FORTY-FIRST.

Spell Constantinople. When this is done, after the speller has gone through the three first syllables,

Con-stan-ti—the other girls must call out—no—no—
meaning the next syllable.   If the speller is not aware
of the trick, she will suppose that they wish her to
believe she is spelling the word wrong, and she will
stop to vindicate herself ; in which case she is liable
to another forfeit.   If she knows the trick, she is con-
vinced that she is right, and will have sufficient pres-
ence of mind to persist in spelling the word, notwithstanding the interruption.   If she gets through it
without stopping, the pawn is restored to her.

FORTY-SECOND.

Take a cent out of a plate of meal, without flouring
your hands.   A cent, covered up in meal, is brought
to you.   You take the plate and blow all the flour off
the cent ; after which you can easily take it up in
your thumb and finger, without getting your hands
dusted.

FORTY-THIRD.

Shoot the robin.   This is done by blindfolding the
owner of the pawn, and leading her to a part of the
room where a sheet of paper or a handkerchief has
been pinned to the wall.   She is directed then to
shoot the robin, which she must do by starting for-

wards, extending her right arm, and pointing her finger so as to touch the sheet of paper. Whenever she
succeeds in doing so, her forfeit is restored. Her
finger had better be blackened with a coal, a burnt
cork, or something that will leave a mark on the
paper.

FORTY-FOURTH.

Walk round the room, and kiss your shadow in
each corner.

FORTY-FIFTH.

Kiss both the inside and outside of a reticule, without opening it. This can only be done when the
drawing-string of the reticule is some distance from
the top, and when the lining appears above it. When
you kiss the lining of the flaps or scollops at the top
of the reticule, then you may be said to kiss the
inside.

FORTY-SIXTH.

Two-pawns may be redeemed at once, by the persons to whom they belong lamenting the death of the
king of Bohemia. They must go to opposite ends of
the room, and then turn round and advance so as to
meet in the centre. One must walk very slowly with

her handkerchief to her face, and say to the other, in a melancholy tone : " The King of Bohemia is dead." The hearer must then pretend to burst into tears, and say : " Is it possible ! Sad news ! sad news !" Both must then exclaim, " Let us cry for the king of Bohemia !"

All this must be performed in a lamentable voice and with disconsolate faces. If they laugh, the forfeits must be redeemed over again.

FORTY-SEVENTH.

When a line is given out to you, answer it with another that will rhyme to it.

FORTY-EIGHTH.

Sit down on the carpet close to the door (which must be shut) and say :

> Here will I take my seat under the latch,
> Till somebody comes a kiss to snatch.

The pawn is redeemed as soon as one of your playmates kisses you.

FORTY-NINTH.

A number of pawns may be redeemed together, by the owners all sitting in a row and playing Mrs

M'Tavish ; which is performed by the following dialogue going round :

" Mrs M'Tavish has fainted away."

" Is it possible ? How did she faint ?"

" Just so."

The speaker then throws herself back, and looks as if she was fainting. The one next to her then, in turn, announces the fainting of Mrs M'Tavish. Thus the play goes on, till all engaged in it have performed the fainting, and this redeems the forfeits. The whole must be done without laughing. The modes of fainting should all be as different as possible, and may be made very diverting.

FIFTIETH.

After a number of pawns have been sold, those that are left on hand may be redeemed all at once, by the whole company performing a Cat's Concert. That is, they must all sing together, as if in chorus ; but each must sing a different song and tune. . One verse will be sufficient.

PLAYS WITH TOYS.

THE GRACES.

Thɪs is played with two small hoops and four sticks. Each player takes a pair of sticks and a hoop, and stands opposite to her adversary. The sticks are held one in each hand, so as to cross ; the hoop is hung on their points, and then tossed over to the other player, who must endeavour to catch it on the points of *her* sticks, having first tossed her own hoop towards her opponent. The hoops are thus alternately thrown backwards and forwards, and received on the points of the sticks, which are always held across each other. Every time the hoop is successfully caught, without being allowed to fall to the ground, counts one ; and the player, who can count most when the play is over, wins the game. To become so dexterous as always to catch the hoop, requires considerable practice. Beginners had better commence with one hoop, only, between them ; as it is much easier than to keep two going at once. This little game affords very good and healthful exercise, and, when well played, is extremely graceful. It is, however, too difficult for small children, unless they are uncommonly alert.

BATTLEDORE AND SHUTTLECOCK.

This game may be played either single or double ; that is, by one or by two persons. The shuttlecock (or bird, as some call it) is a cork, with a bunch of small feathers stuck into one end. The battledore, or bat, is the instrument by which the shuttlecock is struck.

To play single battledore, you must strike or toss the shuttlecock perpendicularly, or up and down; catching it every time on the battledore, which you hold in your hand horizontally.

Double shuttlecock is played by two persons, standing opposite to each other. The battledores are held up so as rather to incline forwards, and the shuttlecock is struck backwards and forwards horizontally, each as it reachrs her battledore driving it back again towards her adversary.

Each player must count how many times in succession she can keep up the battledore, without allowing it to fall to the ground.

LOTO.

A Loto Box which may be had always at the German or French toy-shops, should contain cards marked with figures (as 2, 15, 24, 8, 40, &c.) ; a bag of buttons with figures on the under side ; a round wooden plate to lay them on when not wanted ; and a little basket with counters, which are round pieces of ivory resembling wafers. This game may be played by any number of persons from two to twelve.

A card is laid before each player. The one, appointed to call out the figures, keeps the bag beside her, and, taking out the buttons one at a time, proclaims the number she finds on it. If, for instance, the number announced is 65, each of the players must look for that figure on her card. If it happens to be there, she must lay one of the counters on it ; the basket being placed on the table to begin the game with. If the next number, produced from the bag of buttons, chances to be 18, whoever finds the figure 18 on her card covers it with a counter. If but few are playing, it may happen that none of their cards may contain the figure that is wanted ; in which case, there is nothing to be done but to draw out another button from the bag. The buttons, after having been called, are laid on the wooden plate in the middle of the table, and when all the counters in the basket are exhausted, they (the buttons) may be used to cover the figures on the cards. She, that succeeds first in getting all her figures covered, is the winner of the game. If the company is small, the cards that have been used are laid aside after the conclusion of the game ; and new ones, for the next game, are taken from the box.

When only a few are playing, two or three cards may be allotted to each person. But this considerably lengthens the game, as a longer time is required to look over several cards in search of the right figure, than is necessary when there is only one card. When very little girls are playing, we would recommend that each of the company should have but one card at a time.

DOMINO.

A domino-box contains twenty-four oblong pieces of ivory, each divided into two parts by a line down the middle, and marked with round black spots. Each piece contains spots which designate two numbers, as four and six, three and five, and some have two sixes, two threes, &c.

This game is best played by two persons only, one of whom distributes the dominos with the blank side uppermost, allotting an equal number to each player. The dominos must then be set up on the edge, and in such manner that your adversary cannot distinguish the spots. She, that has not dealt or distributed the dominos, must begin the game by laying one of her pieces in the middle of the table. Supposing that Jane and Lucy are playing, Jane may commence with a piece that contains the numbers five and two. Lucy must then look in her collection for a piece that has on it either a five or a two. She finds one that has five spots on one half, and six on the other. She lays it close to the one that Jane has just played, and in such a manner that the two fives meet each other. The numbers now wanted are two and six. Jane finds among hers a six and four, and lays it next to Lucy's six. Lucy must now seek for a four or a two, as those are the numbers at the ends of the line of dominos that have been played. She finds one with two and three, and places the two next to its corresponding number, so that the numbers now to be play ed are four or three. In this manner the play goes on, till all the dominos have taken places on the board, or middle of the table. If one of the players finds that she is unable to match either end of the row or line, she loses her turn, and her adversary plays instead of her. The winner of the game is she that has first played out all her dominos.

CHEQUERS OR DRAUGHTS.

This game is played by two persons, on a board with 32 black squares and 32 white ones. The pieces (or men, as they are commonly called) are twenty-four in number, one dozen of one colour, the other dozen of another. We will suppose them to be white and red, and that Maria and Louisa are playing. Maria takes the red and Louisa the white men, and they are placed in rows on the black chequers, so as to leave two lines of empty black chequers in the middle of the board, as a space on which to begin the game.

The men can only be moved into one chequer at a time, and from one black square to another. You must always move diagonally or slanting, and never cross over a white square. All your moves must be *towards* your adversary, and *from* yourself. The aim of each player is to reach the extremity, or the farthest squares on the opposite side of the board, and to take as many of her antagonist's pieces as possible. By taking her pieces, you weaken her force ; and, by arriving at the last line on the other side, your men become kings, and are then empowered to move either backwards or forwards ; always however moving diagonally, and only into the next black square.

The players, of course, move their pieces alternately. If, in moving, Maria leaves a vacant black square behind one of her men, and Louisa has a man immediately next to it, she can jump over Maria's man with hers and take him captive. He is then laid aside, and is used no more during the game, except for the purpose of crowning a king. All the taking

9

must be done diagonally, or in a slanting direction, and (except with a king) you can only take towards your adversary. If Maria moves up a man close to one of Louisa's, with a view of taking him at the next move, Louisa may find perhaps that she can save him by filling up the vacancy with another of *her* men. Two men, if left unprotected, can be jumped over and taken at one move, but then there must be a vacant space diagonally behind each. Sometimes, after Louisa has just taken a man, Maria is immediately able to retaliate by at once capturing the victor. This, however, should have been foreseen, and guarded against on the part of Louisa. A man may be saved by moving him in between two others.

When you have succeeded in getting a man safely to the opposite extremity of the board, he becomes a king, and is crowned by placing on him one of the men that has been taken and laid aside.

A king can move and take either way, backwards or forwards; therefore as he has more power than a man, the player who has most kings generally wins the game, or could do so if he manages rightly.

The play is at an end when all your adversary's pieces are taken, or driven into corners from which they cannot move.

If you neglect an opportunity of taking when you have it in your power, you forfeit your own man, and your adversary then removes him from the board. This is called huffing. The first move at the commencement of the game is allotted to each player in turn.

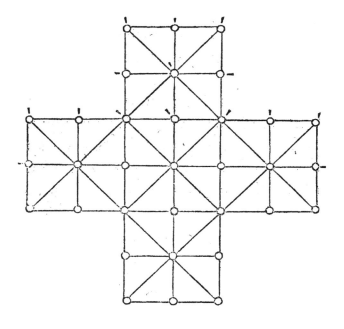

FOX AND GEESE.

This game is played on a board marked as above. Fifteen men (the same as those in chequers or draughts), twelve being of one colour and three of another, compose the flock of geese. The fox is represented by two men placed one on another, (like the king in chequers,) or by a thimble, or something similar. One player takes the fox only, the other has the fifteen geese.

Place the fox on the round spot in the very centre of the board, and the geese at the stations or points marked by dots. The fox can move both ways, either backward or forward. The geese move forward only.

The object of the geese is to pen up the fox so that he cannot move to any advantage. The fox must try to lessen the number of geese by taking as many as he can. He takes by jumping over every one that has a vacancy immediately behind it, and if he succeeds in capturing so many geese that not enough are left to pen him up, he of course wins the game. The geese win, if they can manage to surround the fox so closely that he has no way to get out.

Neither fox nor geese can move to more than one point at a time, and they must always keep along the line.

With a large sheet of paper, a pen and a ruler, it is very easy to make a board for playing this game.

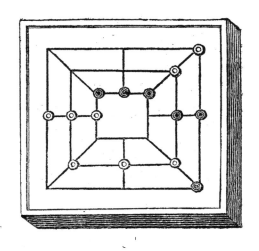

MORRICE.

This game may easily be learned by children of four or five years old. A morrice-board is frequently found on the back of the small German chequer-boards and it is played with the same men or pieces. But if you have no other board for this game, it is very easy to draw one after the above pattern, on a large sheet of paper, with pen and ink, and a ruler. Morrice is played with eighteen men; nine of each colour. The object is to make rows of three men on a line, and to prevent your adversary from doing so.

Susan may take the red men, and Mary the white, but the pieces are not placed all at once on the board, as in chequers. Each player puts down one man at a time alternately, always placing them on the angles, or where the lines cross each other. Three will make a row, if they are all placed on a straight line ; and if cleverly arranged, one man may form a part of two rows.

If Susan sees that Mary has nearly made a row, she may prevent her by interposing one of her own men. If Mary succeeds in making a row, Susan forfeits one of her own men, which Mary takes up and lays aside. In seizing a forfeit-man she must not break one of Susan's rows, if she can possibly avoid it.

When all the men have in this manner been placed on the board, the players may begin to move. All the moves must be along the line, and only from one point to the next, each time. The object is still to make rows, by moving the men to different parts of the board, and intercepting your adversary. Whenever you make a new row, you take up and lay aside one of your antagonist's men. As soon as the number of your men is reduced to two, you may give up the game as lost ; three being always necessary to complete a row.

The writer has seen this game played in the country, by children, who, for want of a better apparatus, had made a morrice-board by chalking the lines on the lid of an old box, using dried beans and grains of corn as substitutes for the red and white men.

JACK STRAWS.

Jack straws of ivory can be bought in little boxes at the toy-shops ; but they can easily be made at home with a small knife and some pieces of cedar, or any other wood that will not break easily. They must be cut into long slips of six or eight inches in length, and the thickness of a small straw ; and each must be marked with a figure, as 1, 2, 3, 4, 5, &c. The little stick, called the picker, must be rather stouter than the straws, and furnished at the end with a hook made of fine wire, or of a bent pin. The jack-straws may be made in various forms, as little guns, swords, spears, axes, arrows, &c. ; on the broad ends of which, the numbers may be marked with pen and ink.

Any number of persons may join in this amusement. She, that begins the play, takes up the bundle of straws in her hand, and then lets them fall in a heap on the middle of the table. She then takes the picker, and endeavours, by its assistance, to lift the jack-straws one by one from the heap, without shaking the pile or disturbing it. As she takes them up, she lays them beside her on the table.

If she shakes the heap, she must then quit playing, and resign the picker to the next in turn, who pursues the game in the same manner, till she is so unlucky as to disturb the pile ; upon which, she also leaves off playing, and resigns the picker to the next.

When all the jack-straws are taken up, the game is over. As they are all numbered, each number counts one.

When the game is finished, each player must add up the numbers of the straws in her own pile. Whoever counts the most has won the game.

LITTLE GAMES WITH CARDS.

GENERAL DIRECTIONS.

There are fifty-two cards in every pack, and of these cards there are four suits ; two red, which are Diamonds and Hearts, and two black, which are Spades and Clubs. In every suit there are ten cards, marked with spots, in different numbers, from one to ten. Those that have but one spot are called Aces.

The Ace of Spades is always handsomely ornamented with the National Coat of Arms, or some other
device. The kings, queens, and knaves, are called
Court Cards. The four kings have crowns on their
heads, and long robes down to the ground. The
queens wear hoods. The knaves have short coats,
which do not cover their legs. In many games, the
aces are considered superior to the kings ; the latter
being above the queens, and the queens are superior
to the knaves.

Previous to beginning the game, the cards are shuffled by mixing them indiscriminately with the hands.
The whole pack or pile is then laid on the table, and,
if all the company are equally expert, they may cut
for deal. If not, the dealing or distribution of the
cards should be allotted to the one that is likely to do
it best. In cutting for deal, you lift about half the
cards from the pack, and look at the bottom after you
take them up. She whose card, on showing it, proves
to be the highest number, takes the pack and deals ;
distributing them equally all round. When the
cards are dealt, (which must always be done of course
with the blank side uppermost,) each player takes up
hers and examines them, taking care not to allow

any one else to see what she has. They had better be assorted, putting all of each suit together ; but this should be done very quickly, always being cautious to hold them so as not to be seen. The proper way of holding a handful of cards is to take them in your left hand, spreading them out like a fan, putting all your fingers at the blank side, and confining them on the face or coloured side with your thumb only. When you are going to play a card, take it out from the rest with the thumb and forefinger of your right hand, and lay it on the table.

You must neither show your own cards nor peep at the cards of your companions.

The cards must always be well shuffled previous to dealing.

EXPEDITION.

This is a very easy little game, and is soon over. We will suppose Mary, Lucy, Jáne, and Susan to be playing. The cards having been well shuffled by Mary, they all cut for deal. Susan turns up a three, Jane a five, Lucy a king, and Mary a seven. Of course, Lucy deals, her card being the highest.   She deals out the whole pack equally, beginning with Jane and ending with herself, and turning up the last card, (which is the ten of clubs,) and laying it in the middle of the table.   In this game, the players do not look at their cards, but keep them before them on the table in an even pile, with the blank side uppermost.

As the card turned up on the table is the ten of clubs, Jane, who plays first, must take a card off her pile, and, turning up its face, lay it on the ten of clubs. It may possibly be the five of hearts, or the three of spades ; but she is to continue to play one card after another, till she happens to come to a ten.   When she has chanced to arrive at the right card, she takes up all that have been already played and lays them aside. Susan being next, plays a card in her turn, which perhaps is the six of diamonds ; and Lucy, who is next, must take cards off her pile, and play them till she comes to a six.   She then takes up those that have just been played, and puts them aside.   Mary's turn now comes, and she plays the four of spades, and Jane lays cards on it till she comes to a four.   The next card that is laid out to be matched is the king of spades, and finally a king is played upon him.

In this manner, the game goes round, and she is the winner who' has played out all her cards first— for instance, Mary

It is to be observed, that the players do not look at their cards, and know not what they are playing till they have taken it from the pile before them and turned up its face.

RECRUITING OFFICER.

This little game is very simple, and can be played by any number.

Deal a card to each of the company, and a card to the board (that is, a card must be laid in the middle of the table), and continue to do so till the whole pack is dealt out, by which time there will be as many cards on the board, as have fallen to the share of each individual, and if there are two of a sort, they must be laid one on another.

Every one in turn must try to match one of the cards on the board by playing on it a similar one from her own hand. Thus an ace must be played on an ace, a ten on a ten, a king on a king, &c. No one

must play two cards at once ; but, if she has two of a
sort like any one on the board, she must not play the
second till her companions have had their turn of
trying to match something.

When all the four cards of the same number are
out, they must be turned down with the blank side
uppermost, to show that there is nothing more to be
done with them.

Whoever is unable to match any of the cards on the
board, loses her turn of playing.

When all the cards on the board have been matched, they must be put aside, and a new board formed
by each of the company shuffling the cards in her
hand, and, without looking at them, dealing one to the
board. The play then goes on as before. She, that
first succeeds in playing out all her cards, is the winner of the game.

TOMMY COME TICKLE ME.

The whole pack having been dealt out, Mary, the
leader, plays any card she pleases, (for instance, a
king,) saying, as she lays him down, " Here's a very

good king for me." Lucy then plays another king, and says, " Here's another, as good as he ;" Jane plays a third king, saying, " Here's the best of all the three ;" and Anne, who plays the fourth king, says, " And here's Tommy come tickle me."

If, when your turn comes, you cannot play the required card, you must say, " It passes me."

If you happen to have in your hand two cards of the sort that is wanted, you may play them both in immediate succession ; and the same if, by a rare chance, you have three.

She, who plays the fourth card or " Tommy come tickle me," takes up the trick, as it is called, and lays it beside her. It is then her turn to play the next.

The one that is out first is the winner.

OLD MAID OR OLD BACHELOR.

This game, when played by boys, is called Old Bachelor, and three of the knaves are taken out of the pack and laid aside ; the fourth knave being retained as the Old Bachelor.

When played by girls, three of the queens must be put away as useless ; the fourth queen remaining in the pack to personate the Old Maid. This game may be played by any number, and the cards are dealt equally all round. Whoever, on looking at her cards, finds among them the queen, or Old Maid, is to keep that circumstance a secret from her companions. She that sits at the left hand of the dealer leads or begins the game, which she may do by throwing down two aces if she has them, or two kings, two tens, or any two cards of the same sort. Her left-hand neighbour comes next, and throws down two nines or two fives. If she cannot play two of the same kind, she must borrow one of her next neighbour on the left hand, who for that purpose lays down her cluster of cards on the table (the blank sides uppermost), and the borrower selects one at random, without knowing what it is. If she finds it the sort of card that she wants, she plays it with the corresponding one of her own. If it is a card that is at present of no use to her, she must keep it for another time, and in consequence loses her turn of playing.

10

The next then may play two fours or two sevens, or borrow (if she cannot play) two that are similar ; and if she chance to borrow the Old Maid, it will of course be useless to her, as there is no other card to match it, the three other queens having been left out of the pack. However, she must say nothing about it. Some one may unconsciously borrow it of *her* in the course of the game.

After awhile, there will be more difficulty in matching the cards, and the borrowing and losing of turns will increase, as no one must play unless they can lay down two that are alike in number. Whoever is the first to play out all her cards, wins the game ; but it is continued by her companions as long as any cards are left, that they may see who has the Old Maid, which will be the last that remains.

The cards, as they are played, are not removed from the middle of the table, but lie there in a heap with their faces upwards, till the game is over.

SPECULATION, OR MATRIMONY.

This game must be played by four persons ; at least it does not go on so well with a larger or smaller number of players.

The cards having been dealt equally all round, every person is to look over hers and ascertain (though without mentioning it) the sort of which she has most. Whoever succeeds first in obtaining all of one sort, wins the game.

For instance, if Mary, on examining her cards, finds that she has a large proportion of spades, she may set her mind on winning the game by collecting a whole handful of spades, and getting rid, as soon as possible, of all her clubs, hearts, and diamonds. To effect this, she begins by taking one of her clubs, or any other card that she does not want, and turning it down on its face, she slips it along the table to Lucy, her left-hand neighbour. Lucy, before she looks at the card Mary has given her, (and having perhaps set *her* mind on collecting none but diamonds,) takes one of the cards *she* wishes to get rid of, and slips it, with the blank side uppermost, to Jane ; and, before Jane takes up Lucy's card, she must slip one of hers that she does not want to Fanny ; who, having fixed on hearts, slips one of her spades to Mary, which happens to be the very thing that she wanted. Mary, before she sees Fanny's card, having again given one of hers to Lucy. Thus the game goes round, and if

Mary succeeds in changing away all her other cards, and constantly chances to receive spades for them, her hand will soon be filled with spades only ; and, as soon as she has completed her suit, she must display her cards and proclaim herself the winner. Perhaps, however, Lucy may be beforehand with her, and obtain a full suit of diamonds, in which case, Lucy wins the game.

If Mary perceives, by the cards that are sent to her, that another person has also fixed on spades, she had better change her mind and set it on hearts or something else, in which she will probably succeed better, as it is impossible for two to obtain a handful of the same suit.

Every one must keep her own secret with respect to the suit she has determined on, and no one must look at the card that is given her, till after she has slipped her own card to her left-hand neighbour.

LEND ME YOUR BUNDLE, NEIGHBOUR.

This may be played by any number. Deal a card to every one, and a card to the board, or table.

Each, in turn, must try to match a card on the board with one in her hand, playing a five on a five, a nine on a nine, a king on a king, &c. Having done so, she takes up both, and lays them beside her, with the faces upward. If she can match nothing from her own stock of cards, she must look out among her companions for a pile or bundle, which they have taken and laid beside them, and which may have on the top such a card as she wants. For instance, if she sees that, by taking one of the piles, she can match one of the aces on the board, she appropriates to herself that whole pile, with no other ceremony than that of saying, "Neighbour, neighbour, lend me your bundle."

Having by this means enabled herself to take a card from the board, (which card she lays beside her with the face upwards on the top of her own pile) she keeps in her hand the bundle of which she has just deprived her neighbour, and uses the cards as she does her own.

If you cannot by any means obtain a card that will match one on the board, that is, if you have none a-mong those in your hand that will answer your pur-pose, and if you see none that you want on the top of any of your neighbours' bundles, you lose your turn and for that time have no chance of playing.

You have not the privilege of using your own pile of tricks or taken cards ; though you may make free with those of your neighbours.

As soon as any one has played out all her cards, the game ceases. The bundles are then examined, and the cards in each are counted. Whoever finds the largest number of cards in her pile is the winner of the game ; therefore, during the progress of the play, every one is glad to accumulate as many as she can, and would be sorry when she is deprived of her bundle by a neighbour, if there was not at the same time something diverting in the coolness with which the thing is done.

When all the cards on the board are taken up or exhausted, a new board must be formed, by each of the players contributing a card for that purpose. To do this, each must shuffle the cards she has in her hand, lay them down blank side upwards, and take out one at random for the board.

FIVE AND FORTY.

This game may be played by any number. It has no resemblance to any of the other little games.

Five cards only are dealt to each person, and then a card is turned with the face upwards and left on the top of the pack. This is the trump card, and all of the same suit are considered superior to the others and can take them immediately. We will suppose that hearts are trumps, and that the game goes on as follows. Lucy having dealt, Anne who is on her left hand begins the game, and plays the six of clubs, which her companions endeavour to take by playing higher cards ; as, in this game, it is not necessary to follow suit, the highest card always taking. Mary thinks she will gain the trick by playing a king, but Jane finally triumphs with the three of hearts, which though a low card is a trump and therefore of more power. Anne hopes to take the next trick by playing the king of trumps, but Mary has the ace and therefore obtains it by trumping higher. Anne had better not have played her king till she had seen that the

ace was out.   She, that happens to have the greatest
proportion of trumps in her hand, of course can get
the most tricks.   Every one lays her own tricks beside her in separate order, and counts them when the
deal is over ;   each trick counting five, and forty-five
being game.   This time we will suppose that Mary
has three tricks ; therefore she counts fifteen.   The
cards are then shuffled and dealt again, the card turned up as trump being a club.   Jane has the most
trumps in her hand, and this time Mary gains but
two tricks, which with three before make her twenty-
five.

Next time, diamonds are trumps, and Mary has
both the king and the ace and two low trumps beside.
She now gains four tricks to her share, which making
her forty-five, she wins the game, none of her companions counting so high.

After this the cards are shuffled, and a new game
begins.   It must be remembered that the highest card
always takes, without reference to the suit ; that she
who has last gained a trick, leads or plays the next
card ; that a trump will take any thing unless it is
itself taken by a higher trump ; and that each trick
counts five.

A CARD HOUSE.

To build a card-house, take two cards and stand them up, so as to face each other, and meet at the top in the form of a tent. Then encompass them with four other cards laid on their edges and representing a wall; and on the top of these, lay two more as a roof.

To build a two-story card-house, place on the first roof two cards in the tent-form, then add the walls and the second roof. In this manner you may construct as many stories as you please, one above another, till the whole pack is built up.

A card-house should be erected on a very steady table, and great care must be taken not to shake it.

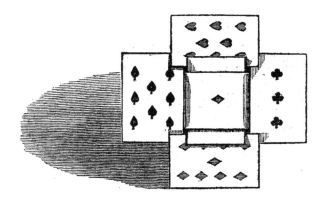

A CHEESECAKE OF CARDS.

This is made by laying two cards across and then fixing round them four other cards; which are secured by raising the corners of the two first, and slipping the last four under them

These cheesecakes (as they are called) may, if well made, be carried about on the palm of the hand without falling apart.

AN EASY TRICK WITH CARDS.

It is best to perform this trick with the black cards or clubs and spades only ; at all events the diamonds must be left out. We will suppose that Jane is the exhibiter. Having the black cards in her hand she must manage (while talking to Lucy with apparent unconcern) to get all the heads or tops of the cards upwards or in the same direction. She then spreading them out like a fan in her hand holds them towards Lucy and desires her to choose or draw out any card she pleases, and to take it and look well at it. Lucy draws the queen of spades, for instance ; and while she is looking at it, Jane dexterously turns all the other cards upside down, so that when the queen of spades is put back among the rest, it of course has the head the other way ; which, however, is unobserved by Lucy, if she is not acquainted with the trick.

Jane then shuffles the cards, taking care not to turn them again so as to get them wrong. She tells Lucy that she can find the very card that she drew out.

She then lays out the cards one by one on the table, looking at them as she does so, and when she comes to the queen of spades she knows it to be Lucy's card because the head is upright, while the heads of all the others are downwards.

This trick, though very simple, excites great surprize in those who have not seen it before.

GAMES WITH HISTORICAL CARDS.

The Historical Games of Philadelphia, Boston, &c. are played as follows ·

In the Game of Philadelphia, for instance, are sixty cards, the labels or titles of which are coloured red, blue, green, and yellow. There are four cards on each distinct subject ; that is, four cards of William Penn, four of Dr Franklin, four of the State-House, &c.

We will suppose the game to be played by Maria, Julia, Emily, and Harriet. The cards, having been shuffled and dealt equally all round by Maria,—Julia, as sitting on the left hand of the dealer, begins by laying down any card she pleases ; for instance, " The Treaty Tree ;" first reading aloud the inscription.   If

Emily (whose turn comes next) has a Treaty Tree card, she also reads it, and lays it down. If Harriet has a Treaty Tree, she does the same ; but if she has *not*, she must endeavour to borrow one of her left-hand neighbour Maria, who for this purpose holds out to her the backs of all her cards, and Harriet takes one at random ; and, if it happens to be a Treaty Tree, she plays it, first reading it, of course. If it is not the card she wants, she must keep it for another occasion, and for the present she loses her turn of playing. Whoever is out first, wins the game.

If any one has two cards of the same title (two Dock-streets, for instance), she must not play them in immediate succession, but keep one till her turn comes round again.

With these Historical Cards any of the other juvenile games may be played,—as, Old Bachelor, Matrimony, &c. omitting to read the inscriptions.

In playing Old Bachelor with the Philadelphia cards, leave out of the pack three of the Dr Franklins, and the fourth will answer for the Old Bachelor.

` In playing Matrimony, you must have but twelve cards of each colour, and leave out all the rest.

RIDDLES.

ENIGMAS, CHARADES, &C.

Enigmas, charades, rebuses, and conundrums, come under the general name of riddles.

An enigma describes the chief properties or characteristics of the thing to be guessed.

A charade must refer to something that has two or more syllables, each syllable being a distinct word. The syllables, when put together, make what is called the whole.

A rebus is founded on a word which may be expressed by alluding to other words ; frequently adding or omitting letters.

A conundrum is a humorous comparison between two things very different in their nature. The re-

semblance is made out by a play on words ; frequently at the expense of a little false spelling, or mis-
pronunciation.

We believe, that few of our young friends will be
displeased at the plan we have adopted of inserting
the solution immediately after every riddle. It will
save the trouble of turning continually over the leaves
and searching out the corresponding numbers.

Where there are several children, each in turn can
take the book and read aloud to the others a page or
two of the riddles, while they, not seeing the answers,
endeavour to guess them.

ENIGMAS.

1.

'Tis true I have both face and hands
And move before your eye ;
But when I move, I always stand,
And when I stand, I lie.

A CLOCK.

2.

'Tis in the church, but not in the steeple,
'Tis in the parson, but not in the people,
'Tis in the oyster, but not in the shell,
'Tis in the clapper, but not in the bell.

THE LETTER R.

3.

There is a thing that nothing is,
And yet it has a name,
'Tis sometimes tall, and sometimes short,
It joins our walks, it joins our sport,
And plays at every game.

A SHADOW.

11

4.

Let those who have skill to make mysteries clear
    Now try to discover my name;
Four brothers I have, and the fifth I appear,
    But our age is exactly the same.
Yet I to their stature shall never attain,
    Though as fast as them always I grow;
By nature I'm destined a dwarf to remain—
    So my riddle you'll easily know.

THE LITTLE FINGER.

5.

If I kiss you by mistake,
What war-weapon do I make.

A BLUNDER-BUSS.

6.

Use me well and I'm every body.   Scratch my back and
I'm nobody.

A LOOKING-GLASS.

7.

What is that which is neither flesh nor bone, and yet has
four fingers and a thumb?

A GLOVE.

8.

What is that which is perfect with a head, and perfect without a head; perfect with a tail, and perfect without a tail; perfect with a head and tail, and perfect without a head or tail.

A WIG.

9.

I 'never was, but always am to be ;
None ever saw me, you may never see ;
And yet I am the confidence of all
Who live and breathe on this terrestrial ball.
The princely heir, his honours not yet blown,
Still looks to me for his expected crown ;
The miser hopes I shall increase his wealth ;
The sick man prays me to restore his health
The lover trusts me for his destined bride ;
And all who hopes or wishes have beside.
Now name me, but confide not, for believe
That you and every one I still deceive.

TO-MORROW.

10.

Pray tell us, ladies, if you can,
Who is that highly-favoured man,
Who, though he has married many a wife,
May be a bachelor all his life ?

A CLERGYMAN, OR A JUSTICE OF THE PEACE.

11.

I'm in every one's way, yet no one I stop,
My four horns each day
Horizontally play,
And my head is nail'd on at the top.

A TURNSTILE.

12.

A word of one syllable, easy and short,
Reads backward and forward the same ;
It expresses the sentiments warm from the heart,
And to beauty lays principal claim.

THE EYE.

13.

I am taken from a mine ; shut up in a wooden case, from which I am never released, and yet I am used by almost every body.

A LEAD PENCIL.

14.

What is that which lives only in winter ; would die in summer ; and grows with its root upwards ?

AN ICICLE.

15.

A word of three syllables seek till you find,
Which has in it the twenty-six letters combin'd.

THE ALPHABET.

16.

In spring I look gay,
Drest in handsome array,
　　But in summer more clothing I wear ;
When colder it grows,
I throw off my clothes,
　　And in winter quite naked appear.

A TREE.

17.

When first my maker form'd me to his mind,
He gave me eyes, yet left me dark and blind ;
He made a nose, yet left me without smell ;
A mouth, but neither voice nor tongue to tell ;
I'm used at night, yet ladies oft, through me,
Although I hide the face, do plainly see.

A MASK.

18.

We are little airy creatures,
All of different voice and features :
One of us in glass is set ;
One of us you'll find in jet ;
One of us is set in tin ;
And the fifth a box is in ;
If the last you should pursue,
It can never fly from you.

THE VOWELS : A—E—I—O—U.

19.

My head and tail both equal are,
  My middle slender as a bee ;
Whether I stand on head or heel,
  Is all the same to you or me :
But if my head should be cut off,
  (The matter's true, although 'tis strange,)
My head and body sever'd thus,
  Immediately to nothing change.

THE FIGURE 8. *If divided, each part becomes* 0.

20.

I have but one eye, and that eye without sight,
  Yet it helps me, whatever I do ;
I'm sharp without wits, without senses I'm bright,
The fortune of some, and of some the delight
  And I doubt not I'm useful to you.

A NEEDLE.

21.

Although a human shape I wear,
  I mother never had,
And though nor sense nor life I share
  In finest silks I'm clad.

By every miss I'm valued much
  Belov'd and highly priz'd ;
Yet still, my cruel fate is such,
  By boys I am despis'd.

A DOLL.

22.

Of a brave set of brethren I stand at the head,
And to keep them quite warm I cram three in a bed ;
Six of them in prison I cruelly put ;
And three I confine in a mean little hut ;
To escape my fell grasp, three reside in the sky ;
And though strange it may seem, we have all but one eye ;
Our shapes are as various as wond'rous our use is,
Of science the source, and the soul of the muses.

THE LETTER A.

*On looking over this enigma a second time, it will be
seen that there are three letters in the word* BED, *six in
the word* PRISON, *three in* HUT, *and three in* SKY. *Of
course there is but one* I *in the whole alphabet.*

23.

Two brothers wisely kept apart,
Together ne'er employ'd ;
Though to one purpose we are bent,
Each takes a different side.
We travel much, yet pris'ners are,
And close confin'd to boot ;
Can with the swiftest horse keep pace,
Yet always go on foot.

A PAIR OF SPURS.

24.

I am a vehicle that's wond'rous large,
But neither coach, nor waggon, ship, nor barge,

Whether sitting, standing, lying,
With you I'm miles uncounted flying;
You hear not a breath while mute as death,
    My journey I pursue;
With a mighty swift whirling, I'm constantly twirling,
    But 'tis all unfelt by you.
Some travel with me, who never can see,
    Nor believe I convey them a yard;
And for years I have taken them,
Nor ever forsaken them,
    And yet claim'd no reward.
And, gentles, against or with your will,
Or sleeping or waking I'll carry you still.

THE GLOBE OF THE EARTH.

25.

I am red, black or white, I am blue, grey, or green;
I'm intended to hide what is meant to be seen;
Like mortals inflexible often am I,
Till by the tongue soften'd I'm brought to comply;
Of prodigal spendthrifts I am an apt token,
I only exist to be ruined and broken.

A WAFER.

26.

I was, but am not—ne'er shall be again;
Myriads possessed me, and possess'd in vain;
To some I prov'd a friend, to some a foe;
Some I exalted, others I laid low;

To some I gave the bliss that knows no sigh,
And some condemn'd to equal misery.
If conscious that we met, and but to sever,
Now say to whom you bade farewell forever.

YESTERDAY.

27.

What force or strength cannot get through,
I with a gentle touch can do;
And many in the street would stand,
Were I not as a friend at hand.

A KEY.

28.

Though I live in a study, I know not a letter;
I feast on the muses, but ne'er am the better;
Can run over English, o'er Latin, o'er Greek,
Yet none of those languages ever could speak.

A MOUSE IN A LIBRARY.

29.

What yesterday was, and what to-morrow will be.

TO-DAY.

30.

Two bodies I have, though they're both join'd in one,
And the stiller I stand, the faster I run.

AN HOUR-GLASS.

31.

What is that which by adding something to it, will become smaller; but if you add nothing will grow larger.

A HOLE IN A STOCKING.

32.

Suppose there was a cat in each corner of the room; a cat sitting opposite to each cat; a cat looking at each cat; and a cat sitting on each cat's tail—how many cats would there be?

FOUR. *Every one of the four would be opposite to each other, might look at each other, and would sit on her own tail.*

33.

Mr Jones told another gentleman that he had six daughters, and each daughter had a brother—how many children had Mr Jones.

SEVEN. *He had one son, who of course was brother to all the six daughters.*

34.

From the depths of the sea, from the foot of a rock,
I'm brought to the earth to do dirty work,
I've mouths to take in all the liquor I meet,
And am given to drinking, though never to eat.

A SPONGE.

35.

I saw a sight the other day,
A damsel did begin the fray;

She with a daily friend did meet,
Then standing in the open street,
She gave such hard and sturdy blows
He bled five gallons at the nose;
Yet neither did he faint nor fall,
And gave her no abuse at all.

A PUMP.

36.

As I was going to St Ives,
I chanc'd to meet with nine old wives.
Each wife had nine sacks,
Each sack had nine cats,
Each cat had nine kits;
Kits, cats, sacks and wives,
Tell me how many were going to St Ives ?

ONLY MYSELF. *As I* met *all the others, they of course were coming* from *St Ives.*

37.

Little Miss Netticoat, with a white petticoat,
    And a red nose;
She has no feet nor hands; and the longer she stands
    The shorter she grows.

A LIGHTED CANDLE.

38.

What is that which goes round the house and round the house and leaves a white sheet in every window ?

SNOW.

30.

Rowly bowly sat on a wall,
Rowly bowly had a great fall ;
Threescore men and threescore more,
Couldn't set Rowly bowly as it was before.

AN EGG ; *which, when it falls and is broken, can never
be restored.*

40.

What is that which in the morning walks on four legs ;
walks on two legs at noon ; and in the evening walks on
three legs ?

MAN. *In infancy he creeps on all fours ; when grown up
he walks erect ; and when old and decrepid he is obliged to
assist his steps with a stick.   This is the famous riddle of
the Sphinx.*

41.

What is that which a pudding has, and which every thing
else that can be found in the world has also ?

A NAME.

42.

There was a man who was not born,
His father was not before him,
He did not live, he did not die,
And his epitaph is not o'er him.

THE MAN'S NAME WAS *NOT.*

43.

A duck before two ducks; a duck behind two ducks; and a duck between two ducks. How many ducks were there in all ?

THREE.

44.

I am small, but when entire,
Of force to set a town on fire ;
Let but one letter disappear,
I then can hold a herd of deer ;
Take one more off, and then you'll find,
I once contain'd all human kind.

SPARK. PARK. ARK.

45.

The beginning of eternity, the end of time and space,
The beginning of every end, and the end of every place.

THE LETTER E.

46.

In comes two legs carrying one leg, which he lays down on three legs. Out goes two legs. Up jumps four legs, and runs off with one leg. Back comes two legs, snatches up three legs, and throws it after four legs, to get back one leg.

A man comes in with a leg of mutton which he lays down on a three-legged stool and goes out. A dog runs away with the leg of mutton. The man returns and throws the stool at the dog to make him drop the leg of mutton.

47.

" What relation is that gentleman to you ?" said one lady to another.　She answered, " His mother was my mother's only child."

HER SON.

48.

I'm longer and longer the lower I fall,
And when I am highest I'm shortest of all.

A PLUMMET.

49.

I'm a singular creature, pray tell me my name——
I partake of my countrymen's glory and fame,
I daily am old, and I daily am new,
I am prais'd, I am blam'd, I am false, I am true——
I'm the talk of the nation, while I'm in my prime,
But forgotten when once I've outlasted my time.
In the morning no Miss is more courted than I,
In the evening you see me thrown carelessly by.
Take warning, ye Fair,—I like you have my day,
But alas! you like me must grow old and decay.

A NEWSPAPER.

50.

A man who was going to cross a river in a small boat had charge of a fox, a goose, and a basket of corn. He could only take one at a time, and was much puzzled how to get them all over, so as to save them from each other ; knowing that if left together, the fox would eat the goose ; and that the goose could not be trusted alone with the basket of corn, which she would certainly devour if allowed to remain with it while the man carried the fox across the river. If the goose was taken over first, it is true that the fox would not meddle with the corn ; but then, after being carried across the water and left with the goose, he would surely eat *her* while the man went back for the corn ; and if the corn was taken first, the fox would demolish the goose when left alone with her.

How did the man manage to convey the fox and the goose, and the basket of corn, across the river in safety ?

He concluded to make four trips, instead of three. First, he took the goose, leaving the fox with the corn. Next he took the fox, and brought back the goose. Thirdly, he carried over the basket of corn, and lastly he conveyed the goose across the river a second time.

By this means the fox was never left alone with the goose, nor the goose with the corn.

51.

Either backward or forward if you take me, ye fair,
I am one way a number, the other a snare.

TEN.　　　　NET.

52.

I'm seen at your dinner ; if I were not there,
But meanly provided your board would appear ;

You seldom invite me to coffee or tea,　`
But never, I'm sure, take your wine without me.

GLAS S

53.

With all things I'm found, yet to nothing belong ;
Tho' a stranger to crowds, yet I'm still in a throng ;
And though foreign to music and all its soft powers,
In songs and in epigrams, ladies, I'm yours ;
Tho' a friend to true glory, I'm ne'er in renown,
Though no kingdom's without me, I hold not a crown ;
Both with kings and with beggars my birthright I claim,
But enough has been told to discover my name.

THE LETTER G.

54.

Form'd half beneath and half above the earth
We sisters owe to art our second birth ;
The smith's and carpenter's adopted daughters,
Made upon land to travel o'er the waters ;
Swifter we move the tighter we are bound,
Yet neither touch the sea, nor air, nor ground.
We serve the poor for use, the rich for whim,
Sink when it rains, and when it freezes, skim.

A PAIR OF SKATES.

55.

I tremble with each breath of air,
And yet can heaviest burthens bear ;

'Tis known that I destroy'd the world,
And all things in confusion hurl'd ;
And yet I do preserve all in it
Through each revolving hour and minute.

WATER.

56.

There is a letter in the Dutch alphabet, which named makes a lady of the first rank in nobility; walked on, it makes a lady of the second rank; and reckoned, it makes a lady of the third rank.

Named, it is DUTCH-ESS.— *Walked on, it is* MARCHION-ESS— *and reckoned, it is* COUNT-ESS.

57.

What is that word of one syllable which, if the two first letters are taken from it, becomes a word of two syllables.

PLAGUE.   AGUE.

58.

Eleven great men ; fifteen celebrated women ; twenty-three extraordinary children ; thirty-two fine pictures ; a new manner of cooking oysters ; the best way of making coffee ; a great improvement in the cultivation of grapes ; ten fashionable bonnets ; and the substance of a hundred books ; may all be expressed by a liquid in common use, and of only one syllable.

INK.

12

59.

I'm seen in the moon, but not in the sun;
I'm put in a pistol, but not in a gun;
I'm found in a fork, but not in a knife;
I belong to the parson, but not to his wife;
I go with the rogue, but not with the thief;
I'm seen in a book, but not in a leaf;
I stay in a town, but not in the street;
I go with your toes, but not with your feet.

THE LETTER O.

60.

In ev'ry city, town, and street,
'Tis ten to one but me you meet;
Sometimes adorn'd in shining gold,
Splendid and brilliant to behold;
And different characters I wear,
A lamb, or lion, buck or bear,
A dragon fierce, or angel fair,
An eagle, or a warrior bold,
These various forms on me behold;
But tho' exalted as a chief,
I'm gibbeted like any thief.

A SIGN.

61.

I ever live man's unrelenting foe,
    Mighty in mischief, though I'm small in size;
And he, at last, that seeks to lay me low
    My food and habitation both supplies.

WORM.

62.

This enigma was written by the celebrated Dr **Byles.**

It is as high as all the stars,
  No well was ever dug so low;
It is in age five thousand years,
  It was not made an hour ago;

It is as wet as water is,
  No red-hot iron e'er was drier;
As dark as night, as cold as ice,
  Shines like the sun, and burns like fire;

No soul, no body to consume,
  No fox more cunning, dunce more dull;
'Tis not on earth, 'tis in this room,
  Hard as a stone, and soft as wool;

'Tis of no colour but of snow;
  Outside and inside, black as ink;
All red, all green, all yellow, blue,
  This moment you upon it think.

In every noise it strikes your ears;
  'Twill soon expire, 'twill ne'er decay;
It always in the light appears,
  And yet 'twas never seen by day.

Than the whole earth it larger is,
  Than a small pin's point it is less;
I'll tell you ten times what it is,
  Yet after all you shall not guess.

'Tis in your mouth; 'twas never nigh;
  Where'er you look you see it still;

'Twill make you laugh, 'twill make you cry;
You feel it plain, touch what you will.

SOMETHING.

63.

Before creating Nature will'd
    That atoms into forms should jar,
By me the boundless space was fill'd,
    On me was built the first-made star.
For me the saint will break his word;
    By the proud atheist I'm rever'd;
At me the coward draws his sword;
    And by the hero I am fear'd.
Scorn'd by the meek and humble mind,
    Yet often by the vain posess'd;
Heard by the deaf, seen by the blind,
    And to the troubled conscience rest;
Than Wisdom's sacred self I'm wiser,
    And yet by every blockhead known;
I'm freely given by the miser,
    Kept by the prodigal alone;
As Vice deform'd, as Virtue fair,
    The courtier's loss, the patriot's gains;
The poet's purse, the coxcomb's care;
    Guess——and you'll have me for your pains.

NOTHING.

64.

FRENCH ENIGMA.

Je suis le capitaine de vingt-six soldats, et sans moi Paris
seroit pris.

THE LETTER A.

CHARADES.

1.

My first is on the reindeer's head,
　My second is a measure,
My total is a favourite dance
　That's always seen with pleasure.

HORNPIPE.

2.

My first is irrational, my second is rational, my third is mechanical, and my whole is scientifical?

HORSEMANSHIP.

3.

Dear is my first when shadowy night is near;
But 'tis my second makes my first so dear;
My whole with decent care my first preserves,
And thus to be my second well deserves.

HOUSE-WIFE.

4.

My first marks time, my second spends it, and my whole tells it.

WATCHMAN.

5.

My first is coarse and homely food,
The cotter's fare, but still 'tis good ;
My second you may quick define,
The place in which we dance or dine ;
My whole, when fresh and nicely cook'd,
No epicure e'er overlook'd.

MUSH-ROOM.

7.

My first I hope you are ; my second I see you are ; my whole I know you are.

WELCOME.

8.

My first is in winter the warmth you desire ;
My second is cold to the touch ;
Both together are cold, yet appear all on fire,
Which has puzzled philosophers much.

GLOW-WORM.

9.

My first has its place by the side of a stream ;
In accents of music my second's express'd :
My whole has the miser's unbounded esteem,
Though oft found relieving where he has oppress'd.

BANK-NOTE.

10.

My first is a colour, my second is rough,
My whole is a story you know well enough.

BLUE BEARD.

11.

My first oft preys upon my second ;
My whole a bitter shrub is reckon'd.

WORM-WOOD.

12.

My first's the foe of rats and mice ;
   My next you'll meet with in a fair ;
My third of various form and price,
   Oft decorates a lady's hair ;
My whole, in foreign climes, is said
To form a mansion for the dead.

CAT-A-COMB.

13.

My first is possess'd of the wonderful art,
Of painting the feelings that glow in the heart ;
Yet had it not been for my second's kind aid,
No respect had my first from a creature been paid;
The name of my whole you can surely reveal,
When I tell you it's chiefly compos'd of bright steel.

PEN-KNIFE.

14.

My first is productive of light;
　My second to wood has affiance;
My whole is high polish'd and bright,
　And my first on its aid has reliance.

CANDLE-STICK.

15.

My first is a pleasant regale,
　Which depends on my second's assistance;
For which, if their efforts should fail,
　My whole may still keep in existence.

FRUIT-TREE.

16.

My first is either bad or good,
　May please or may offend you;
My second in a thirsty mood,
　May very much befriend you.
My whole, though term'd "a cruel word,"
　May yet appear a kind one:
It often may with joy be heard,
　With tears may often blind one.

FARE-WELL.

17.

If my second you can, at request of a friend,
　Then let not my first be preferr'd;

Well performed, (if it answers no permanent end,)
It doubtless will make you my third.

PLEA-SING.

18.

When night brings on her solemn hour,
And silence reigns in awful power,
Then mortals to my first repair,
And bid adieu to toil and care:
My next's for various use design'd,
Yet oft my first you there will find;
Within my whole you seek repose,
Forgetting life and all its woes.

BED-CHAMBER.

19.

My first's a mean and humble bed,
Where poverty reclines;
You'll find my next on bushes spread,
When summer's sun-beam shines.
My whole's a pleasant cooling fruit,
That fails not every taste to suit.

STRAW-BERRY.

20.

My first in your face, has a prominent place
My next in a smile you appear;
A bundle of sweets my whole will complete,
When Flora bedizens the year.

NOSE-GAY.

21.

Behold my mighty first with thund'ring sound
    Hurls forth my second with destructive breath ;
My whole makes legions press the bloody ground
    And close their eyes in darkest shades of death.

CANNON-SHOT.

22.

My first is a term implying a firm
    When it follows a gentleman's name ;
My next plainly tells of a female who dwells
    In seclusion where man never came ;
Martial sounds from my third, redoubling are heard,
    When the demon of war has awoke ;
But what am I doing, this trifle pursuing ?
    For really my whole's but a joke.

CO-NUN-DRUM.

23.

My first upon your table oft,
    At breakfast time has been,
And in your stable rais'd aloft,
    My second may be seen.
My whole contains my first in rows,
And you possess it, I suppose.

TOAST-RACK.

24.

Ages ago, when Greece was young,
And Homer, blind and wandering, sung,

Where'er he roam'd, through street or field,
My first the noble bard upheld.
Look to the new moon for my next,
You'll see it there; but if perplex'd,
Go ask the huntsman, he can show
My name, he gives it many a blow.
My whole as you will quickly see,
Is a large town in Tuscany,
Which ladies soon will recognize ;
A favourite head-dress it supplies.

LEG-HORN.

25.

He who in a ditch doth roll
Till he scrambles out, poor soul,
Rich and clever though he be,
Is my first most certainly.
What good you can, if you are wise,
You will my next ;—my third supplies
A term to abstinence devoted ;—
He who as my whole is noted,
Well may dull and useless be
May it ne'er be said of me.

IN-DO-LENT.

26.

My first denotes equality—my second, inferiority—my third superiority.

MATCH-LESS.

27.

My first some men will often take
Entirely for my second's sake;
But very few indeed there are
Who both together well can bear.

MIS-FORTUNE.

28.

My first is a toy; my second is less than a name; my whole is nothing at all.

FANTOM.

29.

My first denotes my constant place,
My second's what I'm made of,
My whole is useful in a room
Where eating's made a trade of.

SIDE-BOARD.

30.

My first's to object in a troublesome way;
When you come to my house, do my second, I pray;
With nails, saws, and hammers, planes, gimlet, and glue,
A noisy companion—my total you view.

CARP-ENTER.

31.

My first proclaims my whole is near
My second fills the soul with fear,

My whole mid woods and rocks is found,
And gives a fierce and deadly wound.
RATTLE-SNAKE.

32.

Far from the noisy scenes of life,
  Its business and its fears,
My first pursues his tranquil life,
  Through many a lengthen'd year.

Respect and kindness both are due,
  And to my next are paid;
Its wisdom claims the one from you,
  Its weakness needs your aid.

Remote from man, with ivy crown'd,
  On some sequester'd spot;
My whole in ages past was found,
  But now we use it not.

HERMIT-AGE.

33.

In a fit of the tooth-ache my first to obtain,
You'd not grudge a trifle, for sad is that pain;
If nothing you have, it might fairly be reckon'd
A difficult task to discover my second.
Would a man rove about from the line to the pole
To seek a new home, if he were not my whole;

REST-LESS.

34.

My first is an animal scorn'd and abused,
And often in labour and drudgery used,

My next's like my first as one pea to another,
Indeed he's related, if not his own brother.
To make up the third I myself take my place;
And a rare motley crew for my fourth I will trace.
Of soldiers and sailors, and coxcombs and sages,
Both sexes, all trades, all conditions and ages.
I leave to my readers to mention my whole,
'Tis a crime causes horror to thrill thro' the soul.

ASS-ASS-I-NATION.

35.

Arise with my first when a journey you go,
Use my last if your horse is too sluggish and slow;
In the prettiest gardens my whole has a place
From its beautiful colours, its lightness and grace,

LARK-SPUR.

36.

The changing seasons, as they roll,
Confess my powerful first's control;
Nature's unerring laws conspire
To make my second call him sire:
    My whole's but one of seven;
A time when humble christians seek,
With holy zeal and feelings meek,
    The path that leads to Heaven.

SUN-DAY.

37.

My first is nimble, my second innumerable, and my whole
fatal.

QUICK-SAND.

REBUSES.

A DINNER.

1.   A country in the East.

   TURKEY.

   2.   A long-neck'd bird omitting the last letter,—and a small fruit.

   CRANBERRY.

   3.   One of the sons of Noah.

   HAM.

   4.   What no sailor wishes to meet with,—and an inhabitant of the water.

   ROCK-FISH.

   5.   A small fowl—and what all children like.

   CHICKEN-PIE.

   6.   Half of a room under ground—a vowel—and a grain, omitting the last letter.

   CELERY.

7. A cooking utensil—the first letter of the alphabet—and part of the foot.

POTATOE.

8. To strike, changing a letter.

BEET.

9. Half of a word that signifies a tower—and to pinch off.

TURNIP.

10.   To be on an equality—and to cut short.

PARSNIP.

11.   A machine to raise water—and a relation,

PUMPKIN.

12.   A fruit—the half of a pool of dirty water—and a circle, changing the first letter.

PLUM PUDDING.

13.   To chop fine—and the last half of a talking bird.

MINCE PIE.

14.   Swimming—and a country surrounded by water.

FLOATING ISLAND.

15.   Half of a word signifying what is usual—and being late, omitting the last letter.

CUSTARD.

16. What naughty children frequently are—and the best part of milk.

WHIPT CREAM.

17. A running plant, changing the first letter.

WINE.

18. The first syllable of a Persian king—and the first syllable of a town in England.

CYDER.

19. A harbour—and to mistake, omitting the last letter.

PORTER.

A TEA PARTY.

20. A plant that grows only in China.

TEA.

21. Half of a receptacle for the dead—and a gratuity.

COFFEE.

22. Half of an Indian tribe—an interjection—and the reverse of early.

CHOCOLATE.

23. The produce of a plant that grows only in warm climates.

SUGAR.

24. The oily part of a well-known liquid.

CREAM.

25. A fur covering for the hands—and the reverse of out.

MUFFIN.

26. To blow away, omitting the last letter—and the final half of a frill.

WAFFLE.

27. A confused mixture.

JUMBLE.

28. A king's wife—and a confection.

QUEEN CAKE.

29. A familiar name for the squirrel.

BUN.

30. The national dish of the Italians, putting in one vowel, and omitting another.

MACCAROON.

31. The reverse of sour—and what few dinners are without.

SWEETMEATS.

FRUIT.

32. The sea-shore, changing the first letter.

PEACH.

33. A bank to confine water—and what every man must be.

DAMSON.

34. A colour—and a pledge.

GREEN GAGE.

35. A month, omitting the last letter—and a shepherd's house.

APRICOT.

36. An interjection—and to rove.

ORANGE.

37. Half of a Grecian Island—and the reverse of off.

LEMON.

38. A tree that grows best in a sandy soil—and a well-known fruit.

PINE-APPLE.

39. Affected goodness—and to run away secretly.

CANTELOPE.

40. A domestic fowl—and a small fruit.

GOOSEBERRY.

41. A useless dog—and to bluster.

CURRANT.

FLOWERS.

42. The first part of the day—and high honour.

MORNING GLORY.

43. The close of day—to be very formal—and the queen of flowers.

EVENING PRIMROSE.

44. The two first letters of a day of the week—and a part of the face.

TULIP.

45. To start up suddenly—and a crust baked with something in it, omitting the last letter.

POPPY.

46. An ever-green—and a sort of German wine.

HOLLYHOCK.

47. Half of a female christian name—and a little instrument for securing your clothes.

LUPIN.

48. Every day, changing a letter.

DAISY.

49. Forcible or vehement, omitting a letter.

VIOLET.

50. An open carriage—and a community of people.

CARNATION.

51.   A christian name, changing the last letter—and a place that produces metals.

JESSAMINE.

52.   A lady well-known in pantomimes.

COLUMBINE.

53.   A very common female name—and a metal.

MARYGOLD.

HERBS.

54.   A small coin—and whatever belongs to a king.

PENNYROYAL.

55.   Half of a word signifying to bestow profusely—a termination—and the first syllable of a message.

LAVENDER.

56.   A fragrant flower—and a woman's name.

ROSEMARY.

57.   A spice—and the place in which money is coined.

PEPPERMINT.

58.   To be wise.

SAGE.

59.   The measure of duration, adding one letter, and changing another.

THYME.

60.   A season—and to taste agreeably.

SUMMER SAVORY.

61.   To be pleasant—to spoil—and an old-fashioned word for a jug of liquor.

SWEET MARJORAM.

THE UNITED STATES.

62.   A poetical term for the ocean—and a vowel.

MAINE.

63.   The common word for fresh, or modern—and a county in the south of England.

NEW-HAMPSHIRE.

64.   A word derived from the French, and signifying a green mountain.

VERMONT.

65,   A term much used by the southern slaves—to make a choice—and three consonants.

MASSACHUSETTS.

66.   A Grecian island, omitting a letter—and a place surrounded with water.

RHODE-ISLAND.

67. To join—myself—and to divide.

CONNECTICUT.

68. Something recent—and an old city in the north of England.

NEW-YORK.

69. Something fresh—and an English island on the coast of France.

NEW-JERSEY.

70. The name of a worthy and distinguished Quaker—and a word derived from the Latin, and signifying wood-land.

PENNSYLVANIA.

71· Two words that frequently precede French names—and a term for articles of merchandize.

DELAWARE.

72· The name of an English queen—and a country.

MARYLAND.

73. A maiden—and two vowels.

VIRGINIA.

74. A point of the compass—and a female name.

NORTH-CAROLINA.

75· Another point of the compass—and the same female name.

SOUTH-CAROLINA.

76. A name that has belonged to four English kings, changing one letter, and adding another.

GEORGIA.   .

77. The name of many kings of France—a vowel—and a female name omitting a letter,

LOUISIANA.

78· The first syllable of a man's name—the first letter of the alphabet—a sweet herb, omitting a letter—and a vowel.

ALABAMA.

97. A number—three fourths of a bird's dwelling—and to look.

TENNESSEE.

80. A common Scotch word, signifying to know—to inclose—and the letter which is both a consonant and a vowel.

KENTUCKY.

81. An interjection—half a word, signifying lofty—and the same interjection repeated.

OHIO.

82. A savage—and a vowel.

INDIANA.

83. To be sick—a vowel—and a sound, omitting the last letter.

ILLINOIS.

84. A young lady—part of a verb—to taste slightly—and half of a word signifying religious.

MISSISSIPPI.

85. A young lady—and a Mahometan angel, omitting the first letter.

MISSOURI.

AMERICAN RIVERS.

86. To be lively, changing the last letter—and the begining of many Scottish names, adding a letter.

MERRIMACK.

87. An instrument of the greatest importance in making a book—the first syllable of a tall and pointed monument of stone—and a native of North Britain.

PENOBSCOT.

88. Half of a word signifying to crowd together—and the first syllable of a small poem.

HUDSON.

89. The two first syllables of curiosity—and to turn a skin into leather.

RARITAN.

90. The first syllable of uncertainty—three-fifths of a female sovereign—and an old-fashioned name for a woman, omitting the last letter.

SUSQUEHANNA.

91. Two syllables of the berry from which gin is made—the first syllable of a collection of maps—and a vowel.

JUNIATA.

92.   The first syllable of a large troop of soldiers—and the common word for elevated or exalted.

LEHIGH.

93.   The first syllable of a word that signifies but one syllable—a word meaning upon—to be lively, omitting the last letter—a pronoun—and the half of a genteel woman.

MONONGAHELA ´

94.   The first syllable of a well-known nut—a vowel— and a sharp point, adding a vowel.

CHESAPEAKE.

95.   The abbreviation of a common Irish name—beginning of many Welsh names—and to rebuke violently, omitting the two last letters.

PATAPSCO.

96.   A river in Italy—coarse flax—and the first syllable of a small and delicious cake.

POTOWMAC.

97.   A speckled horse—and the monarch of forest-trees, transposing a consonant and changing a vowel.

ROANOKE.

98.   The dwelling of Noah during the flood—a very little word—and a carpenter's tool.

ARKANSAW.

99.   An abbreviation of a man's name—a common word, meaning large—and a useful insect.

TOMBIGBEE.

100.

A VERY GOOD REBUS.

A word if you find, that will silence proclaim,
Which spelt backward or forward will still be the same ;
And next you must search for a feminine name,
That spelt, backward or forward, will still be same ;
And then for an act or a writing, whose name
Spelt backward or forward will still be the same ;
A fruit that is rare, whose botanical name,
Spelt backward or forward is ever the same ;
A note used in music, that time will proclaim,
And backward or forward alike is its name ;
The initials connected a title will frame,
Which is justly the due of the fair married dame,
And which backward or forward will still be the same.

MADAM.

The words that furnish the initial letters are, MUM,—ANNA,—DEED,—ANANA, *(the pine-apple,) and* MINIM.

CONUNDRUMS.

1. Why is a bonnet with a faded ribbon like a lamp burning dimly?

        It wants new trimming.

2. Why are great singers like cheese-curd?

        They require hard pressing.

3. Why is a lawyer like a poker?

        He is often at the bar.

4. Why is a book like a king?

        It has many pages.

5. Why is being in prison like an ink-spot?

        It is hard to get out.

6. Why is going out at the front door in sleety weather, like learning to dance?

        You must mind the steps.

7. Why is a book like a tree?

        It is full of leaves.

8.   What is often on the table, often cut, but never eaten ?
A pack of cards.

9.   Why are friends, separating for a short time, like a pair of scissars ?
They part to meet again.

10.   Why is a looking-glass *unlike* a giddy girl ?
The one reflects without speaking, the other speaks without reflecting.

11.   Why is a counterfeit note like a bar of iron ?
It is forged.

12.   Why is a proud woman like a music-book ?
She is full of airs.

13.   Why is a man that squints, like a needle that cannot be threaded.
The eye is defective.

14.   Why is coffee like an axe with a dull edge ?
It must be ground before it is used.

15.   Why is an expiring candle like a child preparing for a walk ?
It is going out.

16.   Why is a handsome book like an indented servant ?
It is bound.

17.   Why is a slaughtered ox like an ell of cloth ?
It is divided into five quarters.

18.　Why is a pair of skates like an apple?
　　　They have occasioned the fall of man.

19.　Why is a nobleman like a book?
　　　He has a title.

20.　Why is a doctor's prescription a good thing to feed pigs with?
　　　There are grains in it.

21.　Why is a fool's mouth like a tavern-door?
　　　It is always open.

22.　Why is a silk hat like a counterfeit passion?
　　　It is not felt.

23.　Why is a nail like a stage-horse?
　　　It is hard driven.

24.　Why is the British Navy like a printing-office?
　　　It is supported by the press.

25.　Why is the letter P like Lisbon?
　　　It is the capital of Portugal.

26.　Why is a hospital like a key?
　　　There are wards in it.

27.　Why is a madman like two men?
　　　He is a man beside himself.

28.　Why are two giggling girls like chickens' wings?
　　　They have a merry-thought between them.

29. Why is a button-hole like a cloudy sky?
It is overcast.

30. Why is a woman churning, like a caterpillar?
She makes the butter fly.

31. Why is education like a tailor?
It forms our habits

32. Which is the oldest tree in America?
The elder tree.

33. Why, when you go to bed, is your slipper like an unsuccessful dun?
It is put off till next day.

34. Why is a segar-smoker like an author?
He is fond of a puff.

35. Why is a judge like a person reading aloud?
He pronounces sentences.

36. Why is a fool like a very large cask?
He is a butt.

37. Why is a new book like a man that has got through a crowd?
It is just out of the press.

38. What trade is the name of one of the best English authors?
Goldsmith.

39. Why is a fan like a peace-maker?
It allays heat.

40. Why is a reverse of fortune like cleaning fish ?
   The scales are turned.

41. Why is an architect like a great actor ?
   He draws houses.

42. Why is a gun like a jury ?
   It is charged and discharged.

43. Why is a bushel like a well-digested plan ?
   It is a solid measure

44. What trade never turns to the left ?
   Wheelwright.

45. Why is an inferior fur hat like a severe rebuke ?
   It is felt.

46. Why is a hypocrite like an artist engaged in an original drawing ?
   He is designing.

47. Why is a drawn tooth like something forgotten ?
   It is out of your head.

48. Why is a bad epigram like a blunt needle ?
   It has no point.

49. Why is an egg over-done, like one under-done ?
   Both are badly done.

50. Why are handsome women like muffins ?
   They are often toasted.

51. Whether were knees or elbows made first ?
   Knees ; because beasts were formed before man.

52.   Why is a school-boy just beginning to read, like knowledge itself?

He is learning.

53.   What is that which increases the effect by diminishing the cause?

A pair of snuffers.

54.   What is that which, though invisible, is always in sight?

The letter I.

55.   Why is the letter D like a sailor?

It follows the C—(*sea*).

56.   What does a stone become when thrown into the water?

A wet stone—(*whetstone*).

57.   Why is opening a letter like a strange way of getting into a room?

It is breaking through the sealing—(*ceiling*).

58.   Why is a cross old bachelor like a poem on marriage?

He is averse to matrimony—(*a verse*).

59.   Why were Algiers and Malta as opposite as light and darkness?

One was governed by *deys*, the other by *knights*, (*days,—nights*).

60.   If you throw up a ripe pumpkin what will it come down?

A squash.

14

61.   Why is a traveller sailing up the Tigris, like a man going to put his father into a sack ?
>He is going to Bagdad—(*Bag dad.*)

62.   Why is a side-saddle like a four-quart measure ?
>It will hold a gall-on—(*gal*, meaning *girl*).

63.   Why is a pastry-cook like an apothecary ?
>He sells pies and things—(*poison things*).

64.   Why is a coiner of bad money like a line in Othello ?
>Who steals his purse, steals trash.

65.   Why is a pig with his tail curled, like the ghost in Hamlet ?
>He could a tale unfold—(*tail*).

66.   Why is a man marrying a coquette, like a passage in the Midsummer·Night's Dream ?
>"——He gives to airy nothing,
>A local habitation and a name."

67.   What was yesterday, and will be to-morrow ?
>To-day

68.   On which side of the church does the yew-tree grow
>On the outside.

69.   What is that which we often see made, but never see after it is done ?
>A bow.

70.   Why is a poet like a toy ?
>He is devoted to a muse, and delights in fancy—(*amuse—infancy*).

71.   How can a person live eight years and see but two birth-days ?

By being born in Leap Year, on the 29th of February.

72.   Why is taking care of children like wearing spectacles ?

You must keep them before your eyes.

73.   If the alphabet were invited to a party, which of them would come after tea ?—(*T*).

U V W X Y and Z.

74.   What makes more noise than a pig under a gate ?

Two pigs under a gate.

75.   Why is a nail driven tight into a wall, like a weak old man ?

It is in firm—(*infirm*)

76.   Why is a convict just gone to Botany Bay, like one just returned from it ?

He is transported.

77.   What is majesty when divested of its externals ?

A jest.

78.   Why is a prison like a pack of cards ?

There are knaves in it.

79.   Why is an old man like a window ?

He is full of pains—(*panes*).

80.   Why is the letter S like dinner ?

It comes before T—(*tea*).

81.   Why is an andiron like a yard stick ?

It has three feet.

82.   What is the difference between a good governess and a bad one ?

A good one guides miss, and a bad one mis-guides.

83.   What is the difference between twice five and twenty and twice twenty-five ?

Twenty.

84.   Why is a man of an inconstant disposition like a lock and key that fit exactly ?

He is easily turned.

85.   Why is a man suspended in the letter D, what all men wish to be ?

He is in-d-pendent.

86.   Why do white sheep produce more wool than black ones ?

There are more of them.

87.   Why does a miller wear a white hat ?

To keep his head warm.

88.   How many hoops does a good barrel want ?

No hoops.

89.   Where was Washington when he blew out the candle ?

In the dark

90.   Why do you go to-bed ?

Because the bed will not come to you.

91.   Why do we look over a stone wall?
        We cannot look through it.

92.   Which has most legs, a horse or no horse?
        No horse has five legs.

93.   What is most like a cat looking out of a window?
        A cat looking in at a window.

94.   Which is the left side of a plum-pudding?
        That which is not eaten.

95.   What sect will a man belong to if he wears thin clothes in winter?
        The Shakers.

96.   On what tree can you ride from Philadelphia to Pittsburgh?
        The axle-tree.

97.   In what place did the cock crow when every body in the world heard him?
        In Noah's ark.

98.   Why is a jew like the toll-man at a bridge?
        He keeps the pass-over.

99.   What word is there of five letters that by taking away two leaves but one?
        Stone.

100.   What does a man first fall against when he falls out of a three-story window?
        Against his will.

101. What is that which is lengthened by being cut at both ends ?

A ditch.

102. Why is a schoolmaster whipping a boy for telling a falsehood, like the god Apollo ?

He strikes a liar——(*lyre*).

103. Why is Congress like the Theatre ?

It is a House of Representatives.

104. What is that word containing eight letters of which five are the same ?

Oroonoko.

105. What is that which no one wishes to have and no one wishes to lose ?

A bald head.

106. Why is a bad clergyman like a finger-post ?

He points the way he never treads.

107. Why is a coachman like the clouds ?

He holds the reins——(*rains*).

108. Why is Athens like a candle-wick ?

It is in the midst of Greece——(*grease.*)

109. Where did Noah strike the first nail in the ark ?

On the head.

110. Why is a drop of blood like a Waverley novel ?

It is always red——(*read*).

111. What three American coins will make a dollar ?

Half a dollar and two quarters.

112.   If you were up stairs when the house was on fire, and the stairs were away, how would you get down them?

If the stairs were not a way, you could not get down them.

113. What is that which Bonaparte never saw, but which a common man sees every day?

His equal.

114.   If a bird was sitting on a peach in the orchard, and you wanted that peach, how would you procure it without disturbing the bird?

By waiting till the bird had flown.

115.   If you see three pigeons on a roost, and shoot two, how many will remain?

None—as the third will fly away.

116.   What word is that which contains all the vowels, and all in their proper order?

Facetiously.

117.   Why is taking snuff like a ragged riding-dress?

It is a bad habit.

118.   Why is a hat too large for your head, like an old house in an earthquake?

It will fall about your ears.

119.   Why is a cushion stuffed with moss like a bottle of ale left uncorked?

It soon becomes flat.

120.   Why are corsets like Opposition Lines in travelling?

They reduce the fare—(*fair*).

121.   Why is a family of ugly daughters like guns with bad locks ?

They do not go off well.

122.   Why is a lady quitting the arm of an artist like a boat pushing off from the side of a ship ?

She lets go the painter.

123.   Why is a new-married man like a steam-boat ?

The baggage is at the risk of the owner.

124.   Why is a smelling-bottle left uncorked like a hound when he comes to a river ?

It loses the scent.

125.   Why is a liquor merchant like a man of perpetual vivacity ?

He is never out of spirits.

126.   Why is a consistent man like a military coat ?
He is is uniform.

127.   When is a dog's tail not a dog's tail ?

When it is a waggon——(*wagging*).

128.   What is that which unites two and only touches one ?

The wedding ring.

129.   What people can never lie down long, nor wear a great coat ?

Dwarfs.

130.   Why are teeth like verbs ?

They are regular and irregular.

131. Why is a well-trained horse like a benevolent man ?
He stops at the sound of wo.

132. Why is the river Delaware like a fashionable great coat ?
It has two capes.

133. Why is sin like a picture frame ?
It is guilt—(*gilt*).

134. Why is a married man like a student of medicine ?
He must listen to lectures.

135. Why is a poet addressing an ode to a young swan, like a Scotch lawyer ?
He is a writer to the signet—(*cygnet*).

136. What name of an English poet reminds you of the pleurisy ?
Akenside.

137. Why are a fisherman and a shepherd like beggars ?
They live by hook and by crook.

138. What wine is mock agony ?
Champagne—(*sham-pain.*)

139. What check to ambition is there in the meaning of a church weathercock ?
It is vane to a spire—(*vain to aspire*).

140. Why is a very angry man like a clock at fifty-nine minutes past twelve ?
He is ready to strike one.

141.   What is higher and handsomer when the head is off?
A pillow.

142.   If a pair of spectacles could speak to the eyes, the
name of what Greek author would they utter?

Eusebius—(*you see by us*).

143.   Why is a thread-bare coat like a person too soon
awakened?

Both have lost their nap.

144.   There has been but one king crowned in England
since the Norman Conquest.   What king was he?

James the First.   He was king of Scotland,
before he was king of England.

145.   Two letters of the alphabet are such good friends,
that one never stirs from home without having the other to
follow it.   What are those two letters?

Q and U.   Nothing can be spelt with
Q only, unless it is followed by U.

146.   Why is a schoolmaster like the letter C?

He forms lasses into classes.

147.   What difference is there between live fish and fish
alive?

There is *a* difference.   (Because there is
a in fish alive, and not in live fish.)

148.   Why is Philadelphia like a chequer board?
It is laid out in squares.

149.   Why is a nobleman's seal like a soldier?
It bears arms.

150. What is smaller than a mite's mouth?

What goes into a mite's mouth.

151. Why is the letter G like the sun?

It is the centre of light.

152. What question is that which can only be answered by the word " yes?"

What does Y, E, S, spell?

153. What belongs to yourself, yet is used by every body more than yourself?

Your name.

154. Why is a musician like a jailor?

He fingers the keys.

155. When does a barber treat certain letters of the alphabet with severity?

When he ties up queues (*Q's*,) and puts toupees (*two P's*) in irons.

156. Why is a beggar like a baker?

They both need bread—(*knead*).

157. What is that which every living man has seen, but never more will see again?

Yesterday.

158. Why is a fender like Westminster Abbey?

It contains the ashes of the grate—(*great.*)

159. Why is a peach-stone like a regiment?

It has always a kernel—(*colonel.*)

160. Why is an amiable and charming girl like one letter in deep thought; another on its way towards you; another bearing a torch; and another singing psalms?

A-musing, B-coming, D-lighting, N-chanting.

161. What is that which is disgusting to all but those who swallow it?

Flattery.

162. What burns to keep a secret?

Sealing-wax.

163. Why is the king of England like a vane on a steeple?

He is the head of the church.

164. Why are the teeth of an old woman like the visits of persons who dislike each other?

They are few and far between.

165. Why is a gardener selling sweet herbs like a man reading instructive books?

He makes a profitable use of his thyme—(*time*).

166. There is a sort of snuff which the more you take of it, the fuller the box will be. What snuff is it?

Candle-snuff.

167. What is that which occurs once in a minute, twice in a moment, and not once in a thousand years?

The letter M.

168. Why is an active waiter like a race-horse?

He runs for the plate.

169. Why is a drunken man like a wind-mill?
His head turns round.

170. Why is a student of theology like a merchant?
He studies the prophets—(*profits*).

171. Why is the soul a trifle?
It is immaterial.

172. Why is a traveller landing from a steamboat at midnight like an Englishman at a French tavern?
He can get no porter.

173. Why is a hat like a king?
It has a crown.

174. Why is a man who has nothing to boast of but his ancestors, like a potato?
The best thing belonging to him is under ground.

175. Why are dancers like mushrooms?
They spring up at night.

176. Why is a disgraced minister like a melted guinea?
He has lost the king's countenance.

177. Why is a deceived woman like a little girl in leading strings?
She is miss led—(*misled*.)

178. Why are the poker, tongs and shovel like titles of nobility?
They belong to the grate—(*great*).

179. What makes shoes?
Straps; as without them shoes would be slippers.

180. If a little thin man were to dress himself in a tall fat man's clothes, what two cities in France would he resemble?

Toulon and Toulouse—(*too long and too loose*).

181. What is that which is the centre of joy, and the principal mover of sorrow?

The letter O.

182. Why is the letter K like meal?

You cannot make cake without it.

183. Why is a drunkard like a man beating his wife?

He is given to liquor—(*lick her*).

184. Why is a dancing master like a tree?

He is full of bows—(*boughs*).

185. How can great K, little K, and K in a merry mood, make two islands and a continent?

They are Major*ca*, Minor*ca*, and America.

186. Why is a bad piano-player like a bustling housekeeper?

She rattles the keys.

187. Why is Gibraltar like a dose of medicine?

It is hard to take.

188. Why was the celebrated Mrs. Montague like a first rate watch?*

She was always capp'd and jewell'd.

* This distinguished old lady was never seen without her diamonds.

189. Why is death like the letter E ?
It is the end of life

190. Why is a lawyer like an honest man ?
He is man of deeds as well as words.

191. Why is a woman of no attractions, like a plain quaker bonnet ?
She is always without a beau—(*bow*).

192. Why are apothecaries' shops like the gates of death ?
They are always open.

193. Why are clergymen like cobblers ?
They seek the good of souls—(*soals*).

194. In what does a tailor resemble a woodcock ?
In the length of his bill.

195. From whence proceeds the eloquence of an American lawyer ?
From his mouth.

196. Why are geese like Opera dancers ?
No other animals can stand so long on one leg.

197. What are the things that the more you add to them the fewer there will be in a pound ?
Candles.

198. If I kiss you and you kiss me, what sort of riddle do we make ?
A rebus—(*re-buss*).

199. Why ought ladies to be prevented from learning French ?

One tongue is sufficient for a woman.

200. Why is the letter P like uncle's fat wife going up a hill ?

It makes ant pant—(*aunt*).

201. What servant is it, that sits with his hat on before his master ?

The coachman.

202. Why is a farmer surprized at the letter G ?

It will convert oats into goats.

203. Where did La Fayette go when he went out of his fourteenth year ?

Into his fifteenth.

204. Whose best works are most trampled on ?

A shoe-maker's ; because good shoes last longer than bad ones.

205. When is a man over head and ears in debt ?

When he has not paid for his wig.

206. Why is Ireland likely to grow rich ?

It's capital is always Dublin—(*doubling*.)

207. What is it that every one thinks of in telling a conundrum, and every one thinks of in hearing it ?

The answer.

AMUSING WORK.

PINCUSHIONS.

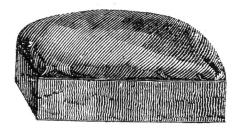

A BRICK PINCUSHION.

THESE pincushions are extremely useful when it is necessary to pin down your work to keep it steady; for instance, in quilling ruffles, covering cord, sewing long seams, hemming or tucking. Being so heavy that they can only be lifted wit h both hands, they sit firmly on the table, and cannot be overset by accident. Screw pincushions, it is true, answer the same purpose; but it is difficult to fasten them to a circular table, or to any table that has not a very projecting edge; and the screws frequently wear so smooth as to become useless. A brick pincushion, when once made, will last to an indefinite period (occasionally renewing the cover), and can be used on any table, in a window ledge, or even on a chair or stool. In a chamber, they can be employed on the toilet like any other pincushion.

Get a clean new brick of a perfect shape, and cut out a piece of coarse linen or strong domestic cotton, of sufficient size to cover it; allowing enough to turn in. Lay the brick in the middle of the linen, which must then be folded in at the corners and sewed tightly with coarse thread all over the brick; making the covering as smooth and even as possible. Then cut out a bag of coarse linen, and fit it to the top of the brick, allowing it, however, about two inches larger each way; or more, if you intend it to rise very high in the middle. Stuff the bag with bran, till you get it as firm and hard as possible. It will require at least two quarts of bran, perhaps more. While doing this, you had better have the whole apparatus on a large waiter to catch what falls. Put in the bran with a spoon, and press it down hard with your fingers.   When the bag is completely stuffed, and cannot possibly hold any more, sew up the open end. Fit the bag evenly all round to the top of the brick, and sew it fast to the linen cover ; taking care to have it of a good shape, sloping down gradually on all sides from the middle.

Sew a piece of thick baize cloth to the linen on the bottom of the brick, and then put on the last cover of the whole pincushion.   This outside cover may be of velvet, silk or cloth.   Fold it under at the corners very neatly, and sew it all round to meet the baize at the bottom.   Then cover the seam with a binding of narrow ribbon or galloon.   If you choose, you can make the cover for the top (or stuffed part of the pincushion) of a separate piece of silk, always taking care to cover the seam with a binding.

A small pincushion may be made in the same manner, only using for the foundation a little flat block of wood, instead of a brick.

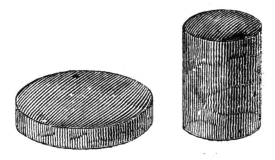

FLANNEL PINCUSHIONS.

Take very long slips of old flannel, cut quite straight and even. For a flat pincushion, the flannel must be little more than an inch broad ; for a tall one four inches. Roll up the flannel as tightly as possible (as they roll galloon in the shops) and sew down the last end so as to secure it. Measure as much ribbon or silk as will go round the flannel, and sew it on. Then cut out circular pieces of silk and sew them on to cover the top and bottom of the pincushion. These pincushions are more easily made than any others, and are very convenient to keep in your work-basket or reticule.

A HEART PINCUSHION.

Cut two pieces of linen into the shape of a half-handkerchief. Sew them together, leaving a small open space at the top, and stuff them very hard with bran or wool. When sufficiently stuffed, sew up the opening and cover the pincushion with silk, sewed very neatly over the edge. Then make the two upper corners meet, and fasten them well together. This will bring the pincushion into the shape of a heart. Put a string to the top. Emery bags are frequently made in this manner. Pincushions should always be stuffed with bran, wool or flannel. Cotton will not do.

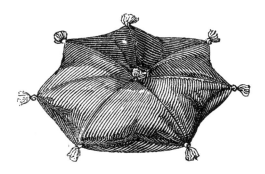

A PINCUSHION IN GORES.

Take some thick new silk, and cut out twelve or fourteen pieces in the shape of gores or long triangles. Half of these are for the upper and half for the under side of the pincushion. Sew them all together on the wrong side, and then sew the top to the bottom, leaving an opening for the stuffing. Stuff it hard with bran. Then sew up the opening. The points of the gores must all meet in the centre, the broad ends going to the outward edge, on which, at the end of every seam, you must put a little tassel or bow, and also one in the centre. The tassel may be made of tufts of ravelled silk. These pincushions are generally for the toilet, and are made large.

A CORDED PINCUSHION.

Cut out two round pieces of linen. Sew them together, and stuff them with bran, so as to form a
round ball. · Begin on the very centre of each side,
and with a large needle lay coarse thread or cotton all
across down to the middle of the pincushion where
the binding is to come. These threads must spread
out from the centre in every direction like rays : the
space between them widening of course as it descends.
Make them very even, and do not allow them to be
loose or slack. Then take a needle threaded with
sewing silk or fine crewel, and, beginning at the cen-

tre from which all the coarse cotton threads diverge,
(they may be called cords) work the pincushion all
round by passing the needle twice under each cord,
taking the stitches very close, even, and regular, and
completely covering with the sewing silk both the
cords and the space between them.   The stitches, of
course, become gradually longer as you go down towards the seam that divides the two sides of the pincushion.   Supposing that you begin with pink silk,
you may, after a few rounds, take another colour, for
instance green, then yellow, then blue, and then
brown.   In this manner your pincushion will be
handsomely striped, and the cords will give it a very
pretty appearance, if evenly laid and well-covered.
When both sides are finished, cover the seam with a
binding of dark-coloured ribbon, and put on a string
and bow of the same.   Always begin and fasten off
in a place that is afterwards to be worked over.

A STRAWBERRY.

This pincushion is made of a piece of coarse linen, about half a quarter square, cut into two triangular or three-cornered halves, stuffed with bran and covered with scarlet cloth; which cover must be sewed neatly on the wrong side, and then turned. The top or broad part must be gathered so as to meet all round, and concealed by sewing on a small round piece of green velvet, scolloped in imitation of the cap of green leaves that surround the stem where it joins the strawberry. The stem must be imitated by sewing on a small green silk cord. To represent the seeds, the strawberry must be dotted over with small stitches, made at regular distances with a needle-full of yellow silk, and close to each yellow stitch must be a stitch of black.

Emery bags are often made in this manner, but of course much smaller; not exceeding the size of a large real strawberry.

A BASKET PINCUSHION,

Get a very small round basket, with or without a handle. It must be closely woven, so that nothing can be seen through its sides. Make of coarse linen stuffed with wool or bran, a round pincushion exactly to fit the basket. Cover the top of it with velvet or silk, and put it into the basket, sewing it firmly to the inside of the rim. This is for a toilet-table.

A BUNCH OF HEARTS.

Cut out ten or twelve small hearts of double paste-board; that is, two pieces of pasteboard for each heart. Cover them with different shades of red silk, crimson, scarlet, and pink, sewing them very neatly at the edges. Sew a string of narrow ribbon to the top of each, and tie the ends of all the strings together. Stick pins round the edge of each pincushion where the two sides unite. These bunches of hearts look very pretty when hung on a toilet-glass.

A BUNCH OF ROOTS.

This is a toilet pincushion. Cut out of coarse
linen or muslin, eight or ten pincushions of the shape
that is called a right-angled triangle, or a half handkerchief; stuff them with wool or bran and then
sew up the ends. Cover them with silk. Fasten
them all together at the top by the upper point or
corner of each, and put a large bow of ribbon at the
centre where they meet.

When stood on the table, these pincushions will
spread out all round, resting on their broad parts.

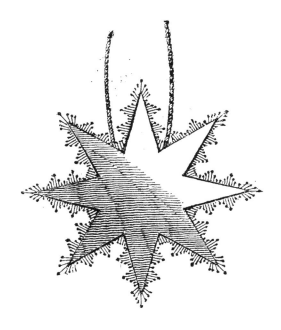

A STAR PINCUSHION.

Cut out two stars of paste-board. Cover them with yellow silk, or any other colour that is convenient. Sew them neatly together over the edge, and round the edge stick small pins. Some of the pins must be inserted deeper or farther down than others, so as to resemble rays issuing from each point of the star. The pincushions are to hang up beside a toilet glass, and are more for ornament than use ; as taking out or disturbing the pins, of course destroys the symmetry with which they are arranged.   However, they are easily made, and to stick the pins in proper order, may afford a few minutes of amusing occupation to a little girl.   They also look very pretty.

A MELON-SEED PINCUSHION.

Make a flat circular pincushion in the manner of those stuffed with flannel, and cover it with silk. Have ready a sufficient quantity of musk-melon seeds, clean and dry.   With a strong needle pierce a hole through the broad end of every one.   String them on threads, or on needle-fulls of buff-coloured silk of various lengths.   Begin at the centre of the pincushion, and sew on the strings of melon-seeds ; every row or circle fitting in neatly between the seeds of the preceding one.   The circle or strings of course increase in circumference as you approach the outer edge of the pincushion.   Do both sides in the same manner.   The last row of seeds that finishes the outer edge must be strung on a fine wire ; and in the finishing row insert between each seed two little glass beads of the very smallest size, and of the same colour as the silk of the pincushion ; blue or pink, for instance.   The outer row, that is, the one that is stiffened with wire, must project a little beyond the edge of the pincushion.

The pins are stuck in the binding that is inserted between the two sides.   Fasten to it a long string of ribbon.

16

A BOOT PINCUSHION.

Cut two pieces of pasteboard into the shape of a boot, in length about equal to that of a grown person's middle finger, or larger if you choose. Cover them with black silk. Put between them several pieces of flannel, cut into the same shape. Unite the two sides of the boot, by inserting, between the edges of each, a binding of black galloon.

When this is done, cover the top or upper part of the boot, on both sides, with a bit of thick buff-coloured ribbon, about an inch or an inch and a half broad, to look like the light leather tops on real boots. Then sew on, at each side of the top, a loop of buff-coloured galloon, to resemble the straps by which boots are drawn on.

The pins are to be stuck in the galloon-binding that unites the two sides of the boot.

A SWAN PINCUSHION.

Get two swans handsomely drawn on Bristol-board or fine white pasteboard. They must be exactly

alike, and represented as swimming, so that the lower
part may be flat, which will enable the pincushion
when finished to stand upright. Cut them neatly
out of the pasteboard. Make a thin flat pincushion
the shape of the swan, growing thinner and flatter
as it approaches the neck. This pincushion must be
made of white silk, filled with a little wool or with
pieces of flannel cut into the same shape, and united
at the two edges with the very narrow white ribbon
commonly called taste. There need be no head to it,
as the heads of the two painted swans will come together at the top.

Then sew very neatly, and with as few stitches as
possible, a swan to each side of the pincushion, uniting them gradually at the neck and head.

A WOMAN PINCUSHION.

Get a small doll's head and arms, of the material called composition. Make a body and upper parts for the arms, of kid stuffed with bran. Then fasten the head and arms to the body.

Make a coarse linen pincushion, something in the shape of a bee-hive, and stuff it very hard with bran. The bottom or lower extremity must be flat, and covered with thick pasteboard that it may stand firmly. Then cover the whole pincushion with velvet or silk, and dress the doll with body and sleeves of the same, or of white satin. The pincushion represents the skirt, and you must sew it firmly to the body, concealing the join by a sash or belt. You may put a handsome trimming on the skirt.

Make a hat or bonnet for the doll's head, and dress her neck with a scarf or handkerchief.

The pins are to be stuck into the pincushion or skirt at regular distances in little clusters or diamonds of four together, so as to look like spangles.

This pincushion is for a toilet-table.

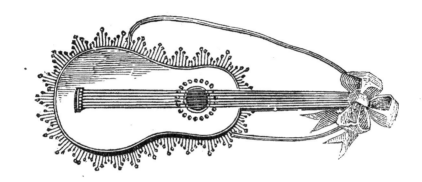

A GUITAR PINCUSHION.

Take two pieces of thick pasteboard, and cut them into the shape of a guitar. Cover them with brown or buff silk. Having put a flannel between, sew them together at the edge. Represent the strings by gold thread, or yellow sewing-silk. At the place where the strings terminate, work a little upright ridge in button-hole stitch or overcast. Fasten a narrow ribbon with a small bow to the top of the handle.

Stick the pins round the edge of the guitar.

NEEDLE BOOKS.

A BELLOWS NEEDLE-BOOK.

Cut two pieces of thick pasteboard into the shape of a pair of bellows, and cover them with silk. Or you may have four pieces of covered pasteboard in the bellows shape, uniting two of each by a narrow ribbon, sewed all round between, to a stuffing of wool. This makes the sides of the bellows thicker and handsomer, but is more difficult to do, or rather more tedious. Get two pieces of cloth ; cut them nearly as large as the bellows, and overcast their edges. These are the flaps for needles. Sew them to one of the halves of the bellows on the inside. Then sew the two sides of the bellows together by a few tight stitches at the bottom or narrowest part, leaving a small open space for the insertion of the bodkin, which forms the nose or spout of the bellows. To secure the bodkin more firmly, make a little loop of sewing silk on the inside of the bellows about an inch from the bottom, and slip the bodkin under the loop and through the aperture below.

Sew strings of narrow ribbon to the handle of the bellows, and tie them tightly over it, when the needlebook is not in use. Stick pins along the edge which forms the pincushion part.

` A THISTLE NEEDLE BOOK.

Take some thick wire, and wrap it round closely
with green sewing silk, or narrow green hank ribbon.
Then cut large leaves of green cloth, and stiffen them

with wire sewed on the under side. Sew the leaves to the stalk. These leaves.are to stick the needles in.

Make a ball of linen stuffed with emery, and cover it with green velvet, worked or crossed with yellow sewing-silk in the form of diamonds. This ball may be about the size of a hazel-nut.

Cut a piece of pasteboard into the shape of a funnel; the bottom exactly fitting the emery-ball, but the upper part spreading out wide. Have also a flat circular piece of pasteboard, cut out to lay on the top of this. Cover both these things with lilac silk, and sew the flat top to the funnel-shaped piece. This when sewed to the emery-ball, forms the thistle flower, which must, when finished, be fastened to the stalk.

Stick pins round the seam at the upper edge of the flower.

This little contrivance answers the purpose of needle-book, emery-bag, and pincushion, and is to be kept in a work-box.

A NEEDLE-BOOK WORK-BAG.

Make a needle-book precisely as described in the
next article. Then take a quarter and half quarter of silk, and cut it in half, as if to make a
square reticule. Sew the two sides together, inserting a covered cord between them. Do not sew the
sides all the way down, but terminate the seams at
some distance from the bottom, so as to leave two

open flaps large enough to conceal the thread-case. Then stitch a seam all across, just above the flaps, so as to form a sort of false bottom to the bag. To this seam sew the back of the thread-case, in such a manner that the flaps of the bag will fall over and conceal it. Sew five pair of ribbon strings on these flaps, so as to tie them down over the needle-book.

Get two yards of narrow ribbon; cut it in half, and run it into the broad hem or case at the top of the bag. Run each ribbon all round the case, the ends coming out at opposite sides to make the bag draw both ways. Tie these ends together in bows.

These bags are very convenient in travelling, or when you take your work with you on a visit.

To cover cord—take some new silk and cut it into long narrow slips, diagonally, or bias as it is commonly called. Sew all these slips together by the ends that slope the same way. Then take some cotton cord, and laying the silk evenly over it, baste or tack it along, so as to inclose the cord. In afterwards sewing this to the straight side of a piece of silk, hold the silk next to you, and let your stitches be very short.

A VERY CONVENIENT NEEDLE-BOOK.

Have ready four pieces of pasteboard about the size of playing-cards, or broader if you choose. Cover them on both sides, with silk sewed neatly over the edges. Get some ribbon of the same colour, and about an inch broad. Sew it between two of the covered cards, so as to unite them all round, leaving only an opening at one end to put in the stuffing. Stuff it

very tightly with wool or bran, which must be press-
ed down with your fingers as hard as possible, and
then sew up the opening.   This makes a pincushion
which will look like a closed book, and the pins are to
be stuck into its edges.   Then get a piece of cloth
nearly twice as large as the pincushion, and overcast
the edges with silk.   Fold it in half, and at the edge
where it is folded, run two or three cases or sockets
for bodkins, which must be prevented from slipping
down too far by a few stitches across that part of the
socket to which the point of the bodkin descends.
The eyes of the bodkins must be left sticking out at
the tops of the cases.

Take the two remaining cards that are covered
with silk, and measure two pieces of silk twice the
size of the cards.   These are for the pockets.   Having made a case in the top of each pocket, and run a
narrow ribbon into it, gather them all round, and
sew them on full to the outsides of these two last covered cards, which must then be sewed one to each
side of the pincushion, having first inserted the needle-flaps.   They must be put on so as to resemble
the covers of a book, with the back of the pincushion
between them like the back of a book.   Sew strings

of ribbon at the two lower corners. At the two upper corners, the ends of the drawing-strings in the top of the pockets must come out and tie. Ornament the back of the book with two bows, one at top, and one at bottom.

The pockets are to contain the thimble, emery-bag, cotton-spool, &c. They will also hold a small pair of scissars, in a sheath. When the thread-case is not in use, it must always be carefully tied up.

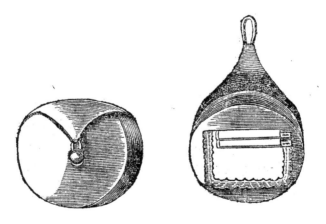

A PINCUSHION NEEDLE-BOOK.

Make a flannel pincushion in the manner already described. Let it be of a flat-sided form, and about as large as a dollar, and an inch thick. Make a round ball of velvet or thick silk, lined with linen and stuffed with emery. You can get emery in small quantities either at the druggist's or at the hard-ware stores. The emery-ball should be about the size of a large hazel-nut. Sew it firmly to the centre of one of the flat sides of the pincushion. Get a piece of pasteboard, cut it of a circular form to fit the flat side of the pincushion, and cover this pasteboard with silk. Then with a piece of silk twice the size of the pasteboard, make a pocket with a case at the top. Gather the pocket, and sew it to the pasteboard as in the needle-book first described. Make an eyelet hole in the middle of the case, and run in galloon, securing it at the ends. This is to draw the top of the pocket.

Prepare two circular flaps of cloth to stick the needles in; overcast the edges and run them together near the back, so as to form a socket for a bodkin. Then sew them on the pincushion; but not of course on the side that has the emery-ball. Then sew on the round piece of covered pasteboard, as a lid to conceal the needle-flaps. To the upper edge of this lid sew a loop of galloon, and pull down the loop to the other side of the pincushion, so as to hitch over the

17

emery-ball, which will thus serve as a button to confine it. This is the fastening of the needle-book.

If you want a string, sew it to the lower part of the
edge of the pincushion.

These pincushion needle-books are easily made,
and are very useful.

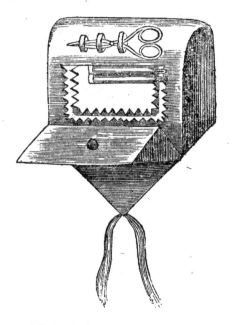

A THREE-SIDED NEEDLE BOOK.

In making this needle-book, the first thing is to form
the pincushion, which is thus constructed. Take

some pasteboard and cut it into three oblong pieces of equal size. They may be about six inches in length, and three in breadth. Cut a small round hole in one of them, and insert in it a socket for a thimble. This socket is sunk in the pincushion, is made of pasteboard, and must exactly fit the thimble, which is to go in with the end downwards.

Cover the three pieces of pasteboard with thick silk, and sew them all together in the form of a prism, or so that the shape of the pincushion will be three-sided. Close one end with a triangular piece of covered pasteboard, and stuff the pincushion hard with wool or bran. Then close up the other end.

Take a double piece of silk about half a quarter of a yard in length, and the width of the pincushion, to one side of which you must sew it. Sew this silk neatly all round the edge, and finish the other end by bringing it to a point. Inside of this silk, put two cloth flaps for needles, with bodkin-cases run in them. You may, if you choose, add three silk straps, under which can be slipped a pair of small scissors. Put strings to the pointed end of the needle-book, and when you are not using it, keep it rolled round the pincushion, and tied fast.

RETICULES.

A DOLL BAG.

Get a doll's head of composition. Make a square bag out of a quarter of a yard of silk, and run a case for a drawing-string at the top. Sew the shoulders of the doll to the bag, just below the case. You can pass the needle through the hole made for that purpose in the composition. Having run a ribbon into the case, draw it up closely round the doll's neck. Make two arms of stuffed linen, and cover them with long loose sleeves of the same silk as the bag. Sew the arms to the inside of the bag, and bring them out at the two slits or openings, that are left at the sides near the case.

Make a very small pincushion of a little slip of flannel, rolled tightly up and covered with silk. It must be of a cylindrical form. Get two small pieces of cloth ; overcast or scollop the edges, and sew them on one side of the pincushion as flaps to hold needles. Then sew on over all a small piece of fur, in such a manner as to hang down and conceal the needle-flaps. When the pincushion is finished in this manner, with the fur over it, it will look like a little muff; and the doll's hands must be sewed fast under the fur to seem as if they were thrust into the muff. The fur must be put on so as to be lifted up to get the pins or needles.

Make a quilted bonnet for the doll's head. She

will look like a lady going out with a cloak and muff.

These bags are very convenient to hang up in the sitting room, as they not only furnish pins and needles, but they afford a convenient receptacle for the scraps and shapings that are left in cutting out work. As the very smallest pieces of linen or muslin are useful to the paper makers, it is wrong to throw them away or to burn them.

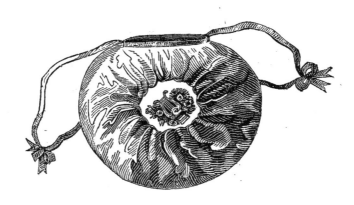

A CIRCULAR RETICULE.

Take half a yard of silk, and cut it into two equal parts, so that there will be a quarter of a yard in each. Sew together the selvage ends of these two pieces so as to make a ring. In the middle of one of the breadths of silk, cut a slit of about half a quarter in length, or a little more. Lay narrow ribbon all round the inside of this slit, and sew it down so as to form a case for the strings; work the eyelet holes on the outside of the case. Gather the silk at top and bottom with four gathering threads, dividing it into quarters.

Prepare two circular pieces of thick pasteboard. They must be about the size of a dollar. Cover them neatly with silk, and mark them into four equal divisions, which may be done with bits of white thread. Then take the silk that forms the bag, and sew it on the inside all round these pieces of pasteboard, making the divisions or quarters match exactly. Run the strings into the case, and the bag will be finished.

These reticules, though they do not look large, will hold a great deal. They may be made very handsome, by covering the two circular pieces of pasteboard with white satin, and painting on them small devices in water colours; something in the style of watch-papers.

A BASKET RETICULE.

Get a small open-work basket of a circular form, and without handles. Then take a piece of silk about a quarter and half-quarter in depth, and make it into a square bag, leaving it open at the bottom as well as at the top. Gather or plait the bottom of the silk, and putting it down into the basket, sew it all round to the basket-bottom. The silk will thus form a lining for the open sides of the basket.

Run a case for a ribbon round the top of the bag.

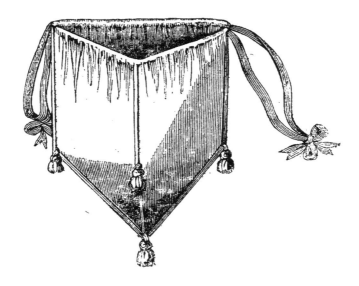

A THREE-SIDED RETICULE.

Cut your silk into three pieces of equal size. Each must be about a quarter of a yard in depth, and half a quarter wide. The sides of each must be straight till within a finger's length of the bottom ; they must then be sloped off to a point. Sew those three pieces of silk together, (inserting a covered cord between the seams,) and make them all meet in a point at the bottom. Put a tassel or bow at each corner, and one at the bottom.

. Hem down the top, and run a ribbon into it.

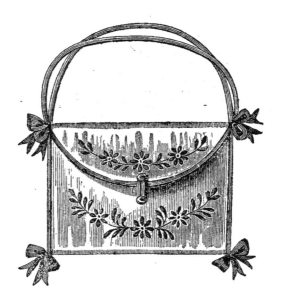

A POCKET BOOK RETICULE.

These reticules are frequently made of white hair-cloth, and embroidered with floss silk; but as these materials may not be conveniently procured, we will recommend thick gros-de-nap, lined with stiff linen, muslin, or buckram. Half a yard of silk will be sufficient. Cut it into the shape of a large pocket-book, and cord the sides and round the flap. Fasten down the flap with two small silk buttons, and a loop of narrow ribbon or galloon. The handles are made of two very stiff but slender rolls of gros-de-nap, cut bias, and filled as tightly as possible with a roll of wadding. These handles must be very firm and hard, and sewed with great neatness. Put ribbon bows at the corners.

A PLAITED RETICULE.

For this reticule, you must have three quarters of a yard of silk, and a yard of thick narrow watch-ribbon, which must be cut into four pieces of equal length.

Cut off first a quarter of a yard of the silk and lay it aside to line the upper part of the bag. Then cut out the bag, dividing the silk into two pieces. Each side of the bag must be the whole breadth of the silk (to allow for plaiting,) and a quarter and half-quarter in depth. The top is to be cut into large scollops, three on each side.

On each side of the bag, baste two rows (one above another,) of even regular plaits, and stitch down on them the pieces of narrow ribbon,—the upper and lower plaits should turn different ways. Then baste on a muslin lining which need not extend to the top, as the scollops are to be lined with silk. Cover a cord and insert it between the two sides of the bag, and all round the scollops at the top. After the sides are sewed together, make a case just below the scollops, and run in the strings. Put a bow of ribbon at each corner of the bottom.

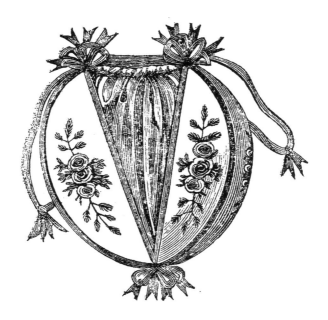

A MELON RETICULE.

A very pretty reticule may be made in this manner. Cut four pieces of pasteboard into an elliptical or oval shape; perhaps they had better be somewhat pointed towards the top and bottom. They should be a quarter of a yard deep, and half a quarter in width. Split two of them down the middle, so as to make four half pieces, and let the other two remain oval. Cover them all with silk, and bind them neatly with narrow ribbon ; or else insert a covered cord between the edges.

Sew the curved sides of the half-pieces to the two curved sides of the whole pieces. This will leave the straight sides of the half-pieces inward.

Make a square bag of a quarter of a yard of silk. Run a case in the top, and gather the bottom so as to draw it up quite close. Unite the bag to the pieces of covered pasteboard, by sewing them all together at the bottom, so that they shall all meet in as small a space as possible.

Make eyelet holes near the top of the outside or whole pasteboards, and when you run the string into the case at the upper edge of the bag, pass the ends of the ribbon through these eyelet holes in the pasteboard, so that it will draw both ways, and connect at the top the silk part of the reticule with the pasteboard.

Prepare three handsome bows of ribbon, and sew one at the bottom of the reticule, and the others at the top. The pasteboards of these reticules may be covered with white satin and handsomely painted. In this case the bags and ribbon should be pink or blue.

A POINTED RETICULE.

Get a quarter and a half-quarter of silk ; cut it into two pieces, after having taken off a slip for the four outside points.   The two pieces are to form the sides of the bag.   They must each be cut out with two points at the top, and one large point at the bottom.   Then cut out the four additional points.   Cord the whole with silk of a different colour, and line them all with the same as the cording.

Then sew the two sides together, inserting a cord between. Next sew on the four outside points, two on each side, so as to hang downwards; finishing their straight edge with a cord sewed also to the reticule. Make a case just below the top-points, and run in a narrow ribbon.

A HALBERT-SHAPED RETICULE.

Take a quarter and half-quarter of silk. Cut off and lay aside a half-quarter to line the top. Then cut out the two sides of the bag, which must be rounded at the bottom, and terminating in a point at the top. It must also be rounded at the upper corner. Line the lower part with muslin, and the inside of the top with silk, sewing a covered cord all round.

Sew together the two sides of the bag, and make a case where the silk lining leaves off.

Get some satin piping-cord, and sew a row of it on the outside of the bag, so as to correspond in form with the shape of the top. Put on two bows of ribbon, one at each side, and run in the strings.

The ribbon and piping-cord had better be of a different colour from the silk of which the bag is made ; for instance, a purple reticule may be trimmed with blue ; a green one with pink, &c.

18

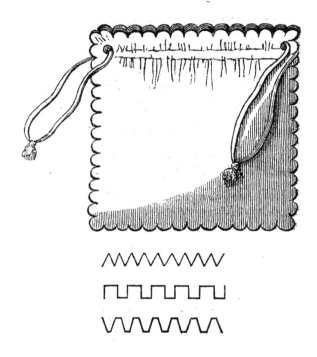

A DIMITY RETICULE.

Little girls will find these reticules very convenient for common use, as they can be washed.

Take a quarter of a yard of fine cambric-dimity, of the very narrowest cord, and split it in two. Cut the shape of a small scollop or point out of an old card or a bit of thick paper. Laying this on the dimity, draw a row of points or scollops all round, taking care not to go too near the edge, and turning the corners handsomely. The drawing may be done with a lead pencil, or the point of a fine camel's-hair brush, dipped in wet indigo or prussian blue. Baste or tack the two sides of the bag together, and following the outline of the scollops, run them along with very neat short stitches; taking care always to stick the needle through both sides, as it is that which unites them.

When you have done running the scollops, cut them out with a pair of sharp scissars, but avoid cutting too close to the stitches. Then turn the bag right side outwards, and with the blunt end of a bodkin poke out the scollops into their proper shape. Get some tape and sew it all round the inside of the bag, about two inches from the top. This will form the case, into which you must run strings of white cotton cord.

These bags may be made of cambric-muslin, or small-figured gingham.

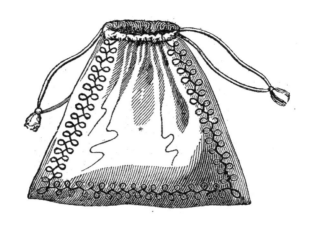

A BRAIDED RETICULE.

Cut out two pieces of new cambric muslin, or fine cambric-dimity. Each piece must be a quarter of a yard wide, and a quarter and a nail in depth, to allow for the case at the top. Have ready a pattern for braiding, drawn with a pen and ink on a slip of thick white paper, and baste it under the muslin, not too close to the edge. Take a piece of narrow worsted braid of any colour you like, (but scarlet, black, or dark blue will be the most durable,) and having wound it in a ball, stitch it neatly with sewing-silk on the muslin; taking care not to draw it too tightly so as to pucker it, and be sure to follow the pattern exactly. Then sew together the two sides of the bag, make the case at the top, and run in a white cotton cord.

When this bag is washed, it must not be scalded or boiled, as hot water will take the colour out of the braid. You may make a very pretty reticule of small-figured blue or pink gingham, ornamented with white cotton braid.

Braiding is a sort of work that can be done very expeditiously. The above are some of the easiest patterns.

VARIETIES.

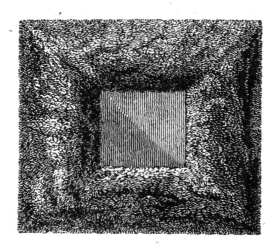

A LAMP STAND.

Procure about a quarter of a yard of very thick cloth or drugget, and cut it exactly square. Then get a yard of wide Brussels carpeting of only two colours, as, for this purpose, a variety of colours causes a confused and indistinct effect, and always looks badly. The best tints for a lamp-stand are shaded greens, varied only with shaded browns. These colours will give the effect of rich moss.

Cut the carpeting into strips about three inches broad. Mark out on the cloth or drugget the space you intend to leave vacant for the foot of the lamp. You can make the marks by tacking a white thread along, so as to form a square. Round the outer edge of this square the strips of carpeting are to be sewed.

Prepare, for the corners, some bits of carpeting, which are to be very small near the white line, and are gradually to increase in size as they advance towards the outer extremity of the drugget. Begin by sewing on these bits so as to fill all the corners with them. Then sew on all the long strips, extending them from corner to corner. Each strip (as well as the corner-pieces) must be doubled or folded in the middle and stitched down on the right side.

When the strips are all sewed on, they must be ravelled or fringed, so as to look like long plush or velvet. Afterwards go over the whole surface with a pair of very large scissars, and shear it as even as possible.

A MATCH BOX.

Get a very small tumbler, such a one as is generally sold for sixpence.   Cover the outside with fine coloured paper, blue, pink, lilac, or light green, pasted on very smoothly and evenly.   When it is dry, paste a border or binding of gold paper round the top or upper edge of the tumbler, and ornament it all over with small sprigs, stars, or spots, cut also out of gilt paper.

You must next have recourse to a colour-box for some burnt-umber, and a fine camel's-hair pencil. The umber is a handsome brown colour; rub a little of it on a plate or saucer, and with the camel's-hair pencil trace a dark narrow line close under the lower edge of the gold border, and also along the right-hand edge of every one of the spots or sprigs; but on no account continue the dark line round both sides of the gold ornaments, as that will destroy the effect. If properly done, the dark brown shade on one side of the gold, will make all the ornaments look as if they were relieved or raised from the surface.

Then fill the box with paper-matches, and keep it on the mantel-piece.

In pasting the coloured-paper on the tumbler, you can leave a vacant space, which may be occupied by a handsome little engraved picture, bordered with gold.

In making matches, cut the paper into long straight narrow slips, an inch or two wide. Fold them two or three times, and stroke them down between your fore-finger and thumb, pressing them very hard with your thumb-nail, so as to make them firm and even.

A RIDDLE FLOWER.

Procure some fine pink, blue, or yellow paper, and cut out thirty-six leaves, all exactly alike. The form must be a narrow oval diminishing to a point at each end ; the size about six inches long, and two inches wide at the broadest part.

Write, in very small neat letters, a conundrum on each leaf, and put the solution on the back, or under side. Cut out of green paper, four large leaves, resembling those of the oak, and write an enigma on each with the answer on the back. Make a fold or crease down the middle of each flower-leaf and unite them all in the centre with a needle and thread ; so that they spread out all round, resembling a dahlia.

For the stalk, prepare some wire, covered with narrow green ribbon wrapped closely round it. With a needle, fasten the green leaves to this stalk, and then put on the flower. In the centre of the flower, put a small circular piece of pasteboard or card, painted yellow so as to imitate the stamina, and sew it on neatly to conceal the place where all the leaves come together. Fasten a similar little piece to the back of the flower where the stem is joined to it.

Three or four of these flowers in a tumbler or flower-glass, make a handsome ornament for a centre table ; and the riddles, if well selected, will afford amusement to visiters.

A DANCING DOLL.

Draw, on fine pasteboard or Bristol-board, a doll about a foot high, and paint her face and hair handsomely; then cut her out. Make, separately from the doll a pair of pasteboard arms, and a pair of legs of the same material; and paint the hands and feet. The doll's waist must be covered with a body or corsage of silk or satin, lined and made shapely with a little wadding. Cover the arms with white sleeves of crape or thin muslin; let them be wide and full, and confine them at the wrist. Sew on the arms to the shoulders or bust of the doll. They should be made as if she was holding out her frock with them.

Prepare a silk skirt, and plait it on to the doll's waist, concealing the join with a belt or sash. You may add an apron of thin crape, trimmed with ribbon, and tucked up at one corner with a small flower.

Put silk shoes on her feet, having sewed on the legs of the doll in such a manner that they will move easily from the knees.

Take a small spool or ball of black sewing-silk. Pass one end of it through the body of the doll, and having made a large knot on this end, tie it to the bar of a chair. Slip the doll along the thread of silk till she is about a yard from the chair. Then place yourself in front of her, holding the spool in your hand; you may stand two yards from the doll. Jerk the thread up and down so as to move the doll, and make her feet go as if they were dancing.

When you are about to put her away, draw in the thread close to her back (the knot will prevent its coming through,) wind up the spool, and lay it with the doll in her box or drawer.

There must be a flat skirt of pasteboard under the silk skirt to shape it out; and to the middle of this pasteboard the legs must be loosely fastened, but not so as to endanger their dropping off.

A JOINTED LINEN DOLL.

Linen dolls, when large and properly made, generally afford more pleasure to little children than those of
wax, wood, or composition, as they can be handled and
played with freely ; and when soiled or injured are easily repaired. No child can hurt itself or its play-

mate with a linen doll, and by renewing the outside covering, and stitching up an occasional rent, they can be made to last for years. We have always observed that they remain longer in favour with their young owners, and continue to give them more real satisfaction, than the handsomest wax doll that can can be purchased.

To make a large linen-doll in the best manner, you will require, perhaps, a gallon of bran, which in the city will cost a few cents, in the country nothing. Before you go to work, collect all the materials, and put them on a large waiter; else the litter on the floor around you will be very great.

Get some coarse white linen, and cut out of it a piece to represent the head, neck, and shoulders of the doll. Then for the other side cut out another piece precisely of the same size and shape. The size of the head, when finished, may be that of a common orange; but the pieces of linen must be quite large to allow for a great deal that will be taken up in stuffing. Then cut out the upper part of the arms (from the shoulder to the elbow) and then the lower part, from the elbow to the wrist; shaping them handsomely. Next cut out the hands. You will not be able to make any tolerable imitation of fingers ; therefore, all you can do, is to round off the hands in as shapely a manner as possible.

Next cut out two pieces of linen for the back and front of the doll's body, and give the waist a handsome tapering shape. Afterwards cut out the legs from the hips to the knees ; and then in two separate pieces, the legs from the knees to the ancles ; shaping them well. Lastly, cut out the feet in four pieces, two for each side.

All these different parts of the doll, must be sewed separately, stuffed tightly with bran, and then strongly sewed up at the ends. They must be stuffed so hard that they cannot be dented.

The head must be made of a good shape and well rounded. To stiffen the neck (which would otherwise droop down, and hang about as if broken) take a smooth round stick, near six inches or half a foot long, and as thick as a man's thumb ; thrust this stick into the neck, among the bran, passing one end up into the head, and leaving enough of the other end to go down into the breast. If the bran has been stuffed in sufficiently tight and firm, it will keep this stick quite steady, and the head will always be erect.

19

The next thing is to sew the different parts of the arms together, so as to make joints at the elbows and wrists; and then cover them entirely from the shoulders to the termination of the hands, with fine white linen nicely fitted. Then sew together the different parts of the legs, making joints at the knees and ancles, and cover them also with fine linen. This outside covering will not prevent the joints from bending. Next, cover the head, neck and breast with fine linen. In sewing the outer covering on the head, great care and nicety is requisite in turning in the folds and wrinkles of the linen. These folds and wrinkles must be so managed as to come as much as possible to the back and top of the head, leaving the face with a smooth and even surface.

When all the different parts are completed, they must be put together, and sewed very firmly with strong thread. That is, the head, neck and breast of the doll must be sewed to the body, the arms must be sewed to the shoulders, and the legs to the lower part of the body.

When the doll is so far completed, her face must be handsomely painted in water-colours; so as to represent cheeks, eyes, nose and mouth; hair must also be painted to look as if curling all over the back of her head, and round her forehead. When the face becomes soiled, it can be renewed by sewing on a new piece of linen, and painting it again.

A linen doll of this description can easily be made to sit alone on the floor, to kneel, and to bend her arms in any position. As has been explained, the joints are formed by making the doll in so many separate pieces, and then sewing them all together. The proportion of each part should be well observed.

You may make gloves for her out of the arms of old kid gloves, and also boots or shoes of the same. Her stockings may be made of the tops of fine old stockings. If properly drest in a nice frock and petticoats (like a baby for instance) this doll will look extremely well ; particularly if her face is prettily painted ; and she will be found an excellent plaything even for a little girl of seven or eight years old, who may take pleasure in making clothes for her.

A COMMON LINEN DOLL.

These dolls are easily made, and answer every purpose for very small children. ● They may be of any
size, from a quarter of a yard long to a finger length.
Some little girls make a dozen of these dolls together
and play at school with them.

Fold a piece of linen or thick muslin in half, and then roll it up as tightly as possible. The upper end of the roll is to represent the doll's head, which must be gathered on the top with a needle and thread and then drawn closely together, and sewed up in the centre. The roll must then be sewed half way down, beginning at the back of the head, and continuing as far as what is intended for the bottom of the waist. From the waist the linen must go loose, and be made to spread out as widely as possible; so as to form something like a petticoat. Cut the linen quite even at the lower edge, that the doll may stand steadily.

Get a piece of calico or gingham for the frock, sew it up behind, and then hem the bottom. Turn in the top and gather it. Put it on the doll, and draw it up closely round the neck, fastening it behind with a few stitches. Form the waist of the frock by wrapping a thread or small string tightly round it, and drawing it in as small as possible.

For the arms, roll up two small pieces of linen, sew them up, and cover the upper part of each with a little of the same calico as the frock, to represent a short sleeve. Then sew the arms to the doll, just above the top of the frock.

A BLACK DOLL

May be made in the same manner as the preceding. The linen part must have an outside covering
of black silk or black canton crape. The frock should
be of domestic gingham or calico, and she should have
a check apron. A white muslin cap on her head
will greatly improve her appearance.

You may make a whole family of these linen dolls,
representing a mother and several children, among
them a baby. A black one may then be added as a
servant.

A PEN-WIPER.

Take two old playing-cards, and cover them on both sides with silk, sewed neatly over the edges. Then sew the càrds together, so as to resemble the cover of a book. To form the leaves of the book, prepare six or eight pieces of canton crape ; double them, and cut them to fit the cover. With a pair of sharp scissars scollop them all round, and then lay them flat and even on the cover, and sew them in with a needle-full of sewing-silk. On these leaves of canton crape the pens are to be wiped. Black is the best colour.

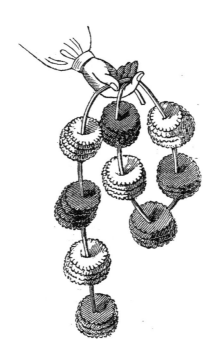

ANOTHER PEN-WIPER.

Cut out a great number of pieces of canton-crape, about the size of half a dollar, and of as many differ- ent colours as you can procure. Lay them evenly in separate piles ; let one pile be black, another red ; some piles blue, and some green. Let there be an equal number of pieces in each pile. Then stick a needle with a thread of silk in it, through the centre of each pile, and fasten the pieces together. When all your various piles are ready, make a small hole through the middle of each, with a pair of sharp-pointed scissars, and run a silk cord through them all, as if you were stringing beads ; arranging the different colours according to your taste. You may make the string of pen-wipers of any length, from a quarter of a yard to a whole yard.

These are very useful to hang over a desk where a great deal of writing is done, and may be acceptable presents from little girls to their fathers.

They will look the better for having the edges scolloped. You may either fasten each cluster of pieces permanently to the string, so as to remain stationary, or you may leave them to slip up and down like beads.

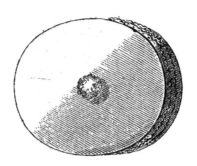

A THIRD PEN-WIPER.

Cut out two circular pieces of pasteboard about the size of a dollar, or larger if you choose, and cover them with silk on both sides. Then get some canton crape ; cut it into round pieces to fit the covered paste-board, and scollop their edges in very small points. You may prepare eight or ten pieces. Put the leaves of crape between the two pasteboards, and fasten them all in the centre, stitching them through and through with strong silk and a coarse needle. Conceal the fastening, by covering it on each side with a tuft of ravelled or floss silk of a bright colour.

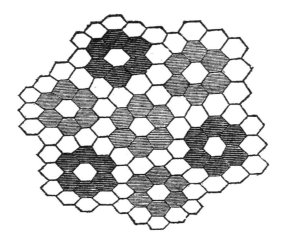

HEXAGON PATCH-WORK.

Little girls often find amusement in making patch-work quilts for the beds of their dolls, and some even go so far as to make cradle-quilts for their infant brothers and sisters.

Patch-work may be made in various forms, as stars, triangles, diamonds, waves, stripes, squares, &c. The outside border should be four long strips of calico, all of the same sort and not cut into patches. The dark and light calico should always be properly contrasted in arranging patch-work.

Children may learn to make patch-work by beginning with kettle-holders, and iron-holders; and for these purposes the smallest pieces of calico may be used. These holders should be lined with thick white muslin, and bound all round with tape; at one corner there should be a loop by which to hang them up. Blower-holders are very convenient for the use of servants, to save their hands from scorching when they remove the blower from the coal-grate.

Perhaps there is no patch-work that is prettier or more ingenious than the hexagon, or six-sided; this is also called honey-comb-patch-work. To make it properly you must first cut out a piece of pasteboard of the size you intend to make the patches, and of a hexagon or six-sided form. Then lay this model on your calico, and cut your patches of the same shape, allowing them a little larger all round for turning in at the edges.

Of course the patches must be all exactly of the same size. Get some stiff papers (old copy-books or letters will do) and cut them also into hexagons precisely the size of the pasteboard model. Prepare as many of these papers as you have patches. Baste or tack a patch upon every paper, turning down the edge of the calico over the wrong side.

Sew together neatly over the edge, six of these patches, so as to form a ring. Then sew together six more in the same manner, and so on till you have enough. Let each ring consist of the same sort of calico, or at least of the same colour. For instance, one ring may be blue, another pink, a third yellow, &c. The papers must be left in, to keep the patches in shape till the whole is completed.

When you have made a sufficient number of the calico rings, get some thick white shirting-muslin, and cut it also into hexagons, which must afterwards be sewed over papers like the coloured patches. Sew one of the white hexagons in the centre of each ring of calico, which must then be surrounded with a circle of white, which will make three white patches come together at each corner of the coloured rings.

In this manner all the patches are put together till the whole is finished. Put a deep border all round, of handsome dark calico, all of the same sort.

Prepare a lining of thick white muslin, and lay bats of carded cotton evenly between, after you have put it into the quilting-frame. In quilting it you have only to follow the shape of the hexagons. When it is taken out of the frame, finish it with two or three rows of running at the edge, which must be neatly turned in.

A COURT-PLASTER CASE.

Cut out of thick paper a model of the case, which is a square of about four inches, with a semicircular leaf projecting from each side; these four leaves when they are folded down shut in the court-plaster.

Lay the model on a piece of fine white drawing-paper, and trace the size and shape with a pencil. Then cut it out. With water-colours paint a narrow border all round, and both on the inside and outside, and also a pretty little device on the back. Write on the inside with red ink these lines ·

"If knife or pin should hand or face offend
This little case its healing help will lend."

ɔSIA information can be obtained
ʋ.ICGtesting.com
he USA
ʹ8190216

ʹ00017B/328/P